The tall woman drove a fist into Doc's Adam's apple, and rammed her knee into his groin.

Then, just as quickly as she had appeared, she was gone.

"Who was that?" Raider asked Welch, the man he and Doc had been talking with just a minute before. But it was too late. Welch was dead with a dagger in his belly.

"I know one thing," Doc croaked in an agony of pain. "She's a bitch. A pure bitch."

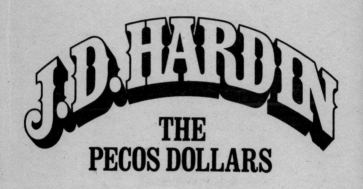

J.D. HARDIN

THE
PECOS DOLLARS

BERKLEY BOOKS, NEW YORK

THE PECOS DOLLARS

A Berkley Book / published by arrangement with
the author

PRINTING HISTORY
Berkley edition / July 1984

ISBN: 0-425-07259-2

A BERKLEY BOOK ® TM 757,375
Berkley Books are published by The Berkley Publishing Group,
200 Madison Avenue, New York, N.Y. 10016.
The name "BERKLEY" and the stylized "B" with design are trademarks
belonging to Berkley Publishing Corporation.
PRINTED IN THE UNITED STATES OF AMERICA

PROLOGUE

Light spilled from the open doors, glinted along the twin barrels of the shotgun. A few feet away, two men grunted, strained sinewy muscles, as they lifted the heavy cartons onto the back of the freight wagon that was pulled up to the loading dock. A fourth man stood back of the cart, in uniform, a pistol riding high on his hip holster.

"Hell of a time to carry coin to the goddamned train," muttered Al Potts, who was inside the wagon, stacking the heavy cartons.

Like the others, he wore a side arm: a Smith & Wesson .38 with a four-inch barrel of blued steel.

"Abernathy said it had to go out tonight on the Denver Pacific," said the guard, a man named Joe Sweeney.

"Well, Abernathy don't have to ride down to the yard in pitch dark, neither," said Potts.

"I ain't got all night, Leonard," said the man standing by the cart. His name was Pat Fairgrove, and he was about to go off shift. He rattled the bill of lading, which was fastened to a wooden board with twine. He was the only man there who would still be alive in the morning.

Leonard Brown said something nasty under his breath and slid another box off the end of the cart. He was married, had two children. He owned one-half interest in the Denver Freight & Cartage Company. He was twenty-nine years old and had worked for Wells Fargo and, for a short time, as a Pinkerton operative. He had a new bride and hated working nights.

Brown was tough as a cavalry boot, and his Smith & Wesson had two notches cut into one of its rosewood grips.

He had carved them himself. He was proud of both the work and what the notches represented: lawless men shot in the line of duty.

"Mary waiting up for you?" asked Joe, shifting the Browning shotgun in his cradling arms. "Or has she got tired of it already?"

"Joe, you got a bad mouth and a nasty mind," said Leonard. "She's waiting for me, and if I'm not in by midnight, she's gonna turn me into a pumpkin."

The other men laughed, letting off some of the tension. No one liked night work in Denver.

The shipment was unusual. One of the guards had failed to show up for work that afternoon. Brown and Potts had to fill in at the last moment. Joe would go with them to the yards, riding in the back of the wagon. Joe worked for the government at the Denver mint and had just come on duty. He didn't like riding shotgun in the back of a dark wagon, either.

Their edginess showed. Leonard pushed too hard and a carton slid off the side of the cart. It hit the dock with a loud clap and every man there jumped.

"Damn it, Len, watch it, will you?" groused Al Potts.

"Hell, watch your end of it, Al."

Pat Fairgrove sucked in a breath, listened to blood pounding inside his ears. His heart raced so that his left temple throbbed like a drum. He let the air out of his lungs in a sigh, and Joe Sweeney shot him a nervous look. Pat said nothing, but he stopped rattling the papers and tried to breathe without making noise. Sweeney was fidgety as a cat in a roomful of rocking chairs, he thought, thus covering up his own jumpiness.

Leonard carried the last box up to the wagon, helped Al shove it into place. Pat checked it off.

"That it?" asked Leonard, knowing it was.

"Just sign this, Len." Pat handed him the board.

Leonard scrawled his name on the bill of lading and did the same for two more copies. Pat gave him one copy.

"You boys ride careful," he said. "I'll see you tomorrow afternoon."

Al buttoned up the wagon, leaving an opening for Sweeney.

"Good night, Pat," said Leonard. "You tell Abernathy I hope he falls through his own asshole and breaks his neck."

The men laughed again.

"He's all asshole," said Pat. "So you'd have to mark a spot."

Sweeney climbed into the wagon. Nobody laughed anymore.

Al finished buttoning up just as Joe found a carton to sit on. Al had stacked them low so Sweeney wouldn't be crushed by a weight shift. Each carton contained freshly minted silver dollars.

Leonard and Al walked to the front of the wagon.

"You drive, Al."

Al climbed up in the driver's seat and unwrapped the reins from the brake handle. The wagon groaned as Brown added his weight to the front seat.

"All set, Joe?" Al called back.

"Set. Roll it, Al."

Pat Fairgrove watched the wagon lurch away from the dock. He felt a sudden pang of emptiness for no good reason. He looked up at the dark, overcast sky. It would rain like hell before morning, he thought, and those boys are going to ride through night as black as a well hole.

The gaslights on Brown's Bluff winked in the inky darkness. The Windsor was still lit up with electric lights, but the secondary streets, as the wagon made its way down Colfax, circuitously beyond 16th and Broadway, were black as pitch. The wagon rumbled on, like a bug seeking its way through an underground tunnel, toward the yards where locomotives hissed and blew white clouds of steam into the Stygian night.

"You coulda picked a more friendly route, Len," said

Potts as they crossed Arapahoe.

"Anybody sees us on the regular route at this hour would wonder why we were out so late and the mint all lit up like a Christmas tree."

"Not likely any of the Larimer or Curtis Street boys would be out on a night like this. It's going to rain like hell in another hour."

"Good," said Brown. "My rain barrel's nigh plumb dry."

The air was close, heavy with a charged dampness. The horses made sounds on the uncobbled street that died away as if they wore cloth on their hooves instead of iron. The wagon hit a rut, and they heard Sweeney curse them.

Al and Leonard laughed.

Then their laughter died on their lips as they saw a red lantern swinging eerily from a corner just ahead. The light seemed to hang in the air without any human assistance, disembodied, floating above the dark street.

"What the hell..." muttered Potts, hauling in on the reins.

"No, Al, keep 'em moving," said Leonard, reaching for the shotgun. Both men stared straight ahead, their eyes riveted on the swinging lantern.

Neither of them saw the limping man at first. They heard an odd scraping sound. Then, out of the shadows, he came, dragging one foot, limping into the path of the horses.

"Look out!" yelled Brown at the man, who seemed oblivious to the danger. Al Potts saw that the team was going to run him down, a crippled man.

"Jesus," he breathed, jerking the reins hard left and snatching for the brake handle.

One of the horses screamed as the lame man twisted and threw up his arms as if to ward off being trampled. The wheels smoked and screeched as the brakes locked up. The wagon lurched into a sickening skid as Potts fought to keep it upright. Heavy crates full of silver dollars shifted in the wagon bed, and Joe Sweeney yelled in pain as two of them cracked his shins.

Leonard, thrown off balance, reached out to grab a hand-hold.

A spoke snapped on a wheel, and Al turned to see a giant, bald-headed man release his grip on a heavy iron flange that looked like a piece of railroad track. The iron shaft was jammed into a wheel. Wood splintered, and the wheel collapsed. Brown was hurled against Potts. Their heads cracked together, and both men saw lights dance like exploding stars in their brains.

Suddenly, other figures appeared alongside the wagon as it ground to a halt, tilted on the broken wheel.

"They got us, Len," rasped Potts, scrabbling for his pistol. A short, stocky man leaped up on the empty seat where Brown had been sitting and grabbed the shotgun out of his hands. A tall figure dashed up and cut the horses loose from their traces, then swung the knife at Potts.

Potts ducked and jerked his pistol free of its holster. A big man walked up casually from where he had been waiting in the shadows of an overhanging roof and calmly fired two shots point-blank into Al's face. Potts didn't even have time or breath to scream. His nose splintered into sharp fragments and his forehead imploded into his brain as a slug smashed the frontal bone like a soda cracker.

Leonard felt the soggy wetness of brains splatter against his bare neck and slide down the back of his shirt. He had seen the big man come up, then ducked when he saw him fire the first shot. The tall man with the knife nodded to the short man with Al's shotgun. The small man swung the butt and cracked Al on the shoulder. Pain flooded his senses.

Joe Sweeney scrambled out of the wagon, dazed by the swiftness of events and the shooting pains in his shins. The bald-headed man was waiting for him. Joe didn't even see the fist coming. It exploded against his mouth, mashing blood vessels, crushing veins, tearing out teeth by their roots. Pain was a sledgehammering thunder that blotted out all reason. Hands grabbed his collar and jerked him down. His knees bludgeoned the ground. When he opened his mouth to gasp his agony, blood and teeth sputtered out, drenching his shirtfront. He felt himself being dragged to the front of the wagon, and he didn't care. He was just a raw, open wound; his hands, emptied of his weapon, were useless, lifeless appendages attached to numb arms.

There were five of them, and none uttered a sound, as if each knew what to do and had rehearsed this scene hundreds of times. Brown noticed all this. Their faces were smudged so that they had no features in the dark. Smeared with lampblack, he figured. He recalled them all as separate individuals, but working precisely, as a fine-tuned machine.

The small man drove the butt of the shotgun into Leonard's groin, and he doubled over in agony.

The bald man threw Sweeney against the front wagon wheel like a broken rag doll. The air went out of Sweeney's lungs.

Then the tall man and the big man disappeared. Leonard heard two wagons—small, light, like sulkies or cut-down spring wagons—come up. The bald-headed man leaned down close to Sweeney's face. He heard him breathing, and then, as Brown watched in horror, he put huge hands around Sweeney's neck and tightened until Leonard heard a bone snap. Sweeney stopped breathing. His tongue swelled outside of his mouth and looked stuck there like a swollen plum.

The bald-headed man went around back and climbed into the wagon. Brown heard the crates of silver dollars being unloaded, quickly, efficiently.

The short man stood over Leonard as if waiting for a signal.

Brown heard his own pulse hammering in his temples. Fear made a queasy soup in his belly. He knew that Sweeney and Potts were both dead. The bandits worked wordlessly, and when they were finished, the two wagons pulled up alongside. They looked, he recalled later, like hearses. Small, black, square boxes on them.

The short man leaped onto an empty seat on a wagon driven by the tall, thin man. He stood up, turned, and triggered off both barrels straight at Leonard. He felt the double-ought buck rip into him. The wagons whispered off toward the swinging red lantern.

Leonard, alive, one arm dangling from his shoulder, half shot away, four ribs broken, his wrist shattered, stared after them, wondering if any of this had really happened.

He kept staring at the red lantern, growing weaker as he felt part of him leaking away.

Now it was perfectly still, and the lantern, still swinging, seemed to bathe the night in blood.

CHAPTER ONE

Josiah Benedict Abernathy, general manager of the Denver Mint, had a stomachache and a scowl on his face. Neither condition was related to the other. His stomachache was a perpetual reminder of ulcers that had blistered the lining of his belly a few months after the bandits had removed over one hundred thousand dollars of Morgan silver dollars from the Denver Freight & Cartage Company wagon. The scowl was for the man standing in front of his desk. He was tall, with shoulders as wide and straight as general's boards, and he sported a thick black mustache that seemed as heavy and solid as wrought iron. He towered above Abernathy, with a coal-black Stetson on his head and eyes even blacker, fixing him like the dark holes of gun barrels.

"Mr. Raider? Pinkerton?"

"Raider. No 'mister.' And I ain't Pinkerton."

"You are from Pinkerton's?"

"I work for the agency. Abernathy?"

"I don't . . . Yes, I'm Josiah Abernathy, but I expected . . ."

Raider, his face burnished copper from sun and wind, his cowhide jacket rank and tawn as a desert, let out a great sigh. As if he had faced many such men before. As if Abernathy was just another bug to swat and wipe away.

"You expected a man in a fine suit," he said, "with good manners and a degree in law. You got me."

"Well, I . . . Do you have credentials?"

Raider rested a hand on the butt of his Remington .44. It was a place to rest his hand after shifting his weight in the calfskin Middleton boots he wore. There was no threat in his gesture. It was natural to him. His dark eyes narrowed and he seemed to grow taller as he looked down at Josiah Abernathy.

"Listen, Abernathy. I wouldn't have been let in here if I wasn't who I said I was and sent here by the Pinkerton Agency."

"Hmm, ah, yes. Well, I have instructions to show you around."

"I want to talk to Patrick Fairgrove."

"The guard. Yes, I've asked him to meet us. Come. We'll start at his station."

Fairgrove was waiting for them at the end of a long corridor. A barred cage guarded a door to the mint's inner sanctum. He stood at attention when Abernathy drew near. His uniform was wrinkled but spotless. Raider looked into dull nervous eyes.

Abernathy made the introductions as though it was something distastefully beneath him.

"You talked to Leonard Brown before he died?"

"I . . . I did. He was dying. I was off duty but heard shots on my way home. Len—Leonard—was just about gone."

"But he could talk?"

"Some."

"He recognize any of them?"

"No. But he gave me descriptions. I put it all in the report."

"I read it," said Raider dryly. "Not much there. A tall man, a big man, a short man, a bald man, and a man with a limp. What the hell was this, a circus?"

"Listen, mister. Al and Len and Sweeney were good men. You don't joke about them."

"I wasn't joking. Any of those descriptions make sense to you? You know anybody who's bald, who limps, who's tall, short, or big?"

Fairgrove looked at Abernathy with pleading eyes. Abernathy turned away quickly and shifted his weight, as though impatient to be elsewhere.

"Could be anybody. Nobody I know. Who could kill like that? So quick, so merciless?"

Raider had heard enough.

"Just about anybody who wanted a hundred thousand in silver bad enough."

Abernathy led the way past the guard's station.

A pretty, rosy-cheeked woman called out to him. She came running down the corridor carrying a sheaf of papers and a small wooden box.

"Mr. Abernathy, I've got the things you wanted." She was out of breath, petite in her severe, high-collared dress. Raider couldn't see her ankles. He tried to, but the dress was too long. It was a pale blue dress and matched her eyes. She had coal-black hair and dimples framing her mouth. The dress seemed a size too small at the bodice. He imagined he could see nipples pressing against the cloth.

"Ah yes, Mr. Raider. You might need to see these coins. I had two struck for you and your partner."

"Partner?"

"I was told that two of you would be working on this case."

"Shit," said Raider.

The young woman's face flushed a pale crimson.

"That will be all, Miss Logan," said Abernathy quickly.

"Yes, sir."

Abernathy handed Raider the box. Raider stared after the girl, watching her buttocks bob beneath her frock. He didn't see the box or take it. Abernathy cleared his throat.

"Sir?" said Abernathy.

"Yeah," said Raider, as the girl disappeared around a corner.

He saw the proffered box then and took it. He slipped the brass latch and opened it. The two silver dollars lay on velvet. They were shiny and new, with an idealized woman's head on one coin, an eagle on the other, which had the obverse side turned up.

The date under the head was 1891.

"What do you think?" asked Abernathy.

"She sure looks cute when she blushes."

"No, not that."

"Well, she's got a nice ass. . . ."

"Mr. Raider! I'm talking about the coins."

"Oh, yeah. Two years old. These like the ones that were stolen?"

"Yes. I had these struck so you'd know what you were looking for. So far none have turned up, and we didn't mint any after the robbery."

"No new silver dollars?"

"None like those. Morgans. Special dies."

"Morgans?"

"George T. Morgan, an artist. Engraver."

"Oh, yeah. Look, Mr. Abernathy, I've got some things to do. I'll look around your place another time."

"I see. When?"

"Tomorrow, next day. I'll keep these coins, see if any turn up."

Abernathy could barely conceal his disappointment. He felt as if he was being dismissed by this unkempt, ungentlemanly fellow.

"Very well. I'll show you out."

"I can find my way."

Raider scooped the coins out of their case and handed the box to Abernathy. He shoved the dollars in his pocket and turned on his heel. Abernathy's mouth dropped open. Pat Fairgrove let Raider through.

"Anybody quit the mint the day of the robbery?" asked Raider.

"Well, I don't rightly know. Maybe. Abernathy would know."

"Yeah, he would."

Raider walked past Abernathy's office and some others. He looked in every one but didn't see the girl again. Outside, he walked down Colfax to Curtis Street. Denver was busy. Building, growing. He could think of eight hundred places he'd rather be. His horse was boarded down at a stable on the end of Larimer, but he'd gotten a room at a hotel on

Curtis. There he was closer to the main part of town. And it was neither fancy nor as decrepit as the fleabags on Larimer or Arapahoe.

He knew someone had followed him from the mint.

At first it had been just a feeling, then something he knew for certain. He let whoever it was come on, catching only a shadowy glimpse of someone ducking between buildings whenever he turned his head. He couldn't tell if his shadow was a man or a woman. But whoever it was wasn't very good at tailing.

Raider made two stops before he got to the Curtis Hotel. He bought some powders for his stomach at an apothecary shop, and a bottle of whiskey from a spirits shop. Ever since meeting Abernathy his stomach had been boiling like a potful of sour turnips. The man irritated him. The whole goddamned case irritated him. Two years ago five men had robbed a freight outfit and stole a hundred thousand dollars worth of silver cartwheels. Now they brought in the Pinkertons. On a cold trail.

And what Abernathy had said about a partner topped off the afternoon. The only man he worked with was Doc Weatherbee, and he had hoped that Doc would stay out of this one. This was a gravy assignment. No clues, no suspects, and no sign of the loot. Long gone. He could kill a month or so on it and get back on his feed. It was probably an inside job and no way to prove it. Wagner had sent a skinny little dossier on the case and told him by telegram to get on it. It was such a bad case he figured the Pinkertons wouldn't waste more than one man on it. The eyewitness account was secondhand and probably of not much account.

Raider strode through the lobby of the Curtis Hotel and picked up his key at the desk.

"Anyone asks for me, let 'em up," he told the clerk.

"Are you expecting someone?"

"No, but let 'em up anyway, and if you got a sawbones stayin' here, you might tell him to get his bag ready."

"Huh?"

Raider took the stairs two at a time. He shoved the key

into the lock of Room 6. He already knew that it would fit Rooms 8, 10, and 12.

He left the door unlocked, put the whiskey on the table, and poured a glass of murky water from the cracked and stained porcelain pitcher on the highboy. He dropped some powders into the glass and swirled them around. He swallowed the concoction, which tasted like alkali and dried horseradish, and he managed to keep it down.

Then he walked to the door and waited for it to open. When it did, he would be behind it, ready.

The door didn't open.

But someone knocked.

Four taps, all soft.

"Come in," he said, his eyes cold as the eyes of a hunting cat.

The handle turned slowly. Then stopped.

Raider heard someone sigh or let out a breath on the other side. He waited. Seconds ticked by. Then he heard footsteps walking away.

Quickly he jerked open the door.

He dashed into the hall and lashed out a hand at the retreating figure. His grasp enclosed a small wrist. He jerked, spinning the person around to face him.

"Oh!"

The woman's eyes widened in fright beneath the veil she wore.

"Who the hell are you, lady?"

"Please, I . . . I shouldn't have come here. Let me go."

"Not until you tell me why you've been following me."

"Oh, dear."

He dragged her into the room and kicked the door shut. The woman was young and handsome. She might have been pretty, but he could see only the bare outline of her face. The rest of it was concealed behind the veil and under a bonnet. She wore black, and the clothes were none too new.

"What are you, a widow?"

"Yes," she murmured.

"Name?"

"Mary. Mary Brown."

She let out a sigh.

"Sit down, Mary Brown, and tell me why all the secrecy. You knew I was at the mint and you followed me here. Something on your mind?"

Mary did not sit down.

Instead, she slipped off her bonnet and peeled back the veil.

Raider wasn't prepared for the beautiful woman under all that gauze and sunshade. Her face was pear-shaped, the eyes blue as a Kansas sky, her lips full and provocative. Her complexion was peaches and cream, like he remembered it on his mother's table back in Arkansas.

"I want you to find them, Raider. Kill them. Shoot them down."

Her eyes flashed and did not make her look unbecoming.

Raider sat down on the bed and dangled a leg over the side. He pushed his hat back from his forehead.

"You Leonard Brown's widow?"

"Yes."

"I didn't know him. He only worked for the Pinkerton Agency a short time. Before Allan died."

"I know. Mr. Pinkerton was a friend of my family. I . . . I know William pretty well. I've lost touch with Robert. He and I didn't get along well. My father admired Allan, grew up with him in Glasgow. My father is—was—Daniel McDougal."

"I see. I knew Dan. Sorry to hear about his death. He helped old Pinkerton back in Dundee when he was a Chicago sheriff."

"Yes. Now I've lost my father and my husband. Len and I have two children, a boy and a girl."

Raider began to get an inkling as to why the Pinkertons were on the case. Allan had died in '85. Leonard Brown had left the agency shortly afterwards. That much was in the dossier. He was sure William Pinkerton, one of Allan's sons, hadn't put him on the case because an ex-Pinkerton had been killed. Or maybe he had. The Pinkertons were all quirky.

"I'm sorry, Mrs. Brown, but I think you're in for a disappointment. The trail's old and probably faded out. No one's supposed to know I'm on this. You put William up to it?"

"I, well, I used some influence in Washington. John Sherman was a friend of my father's and so was Charles Folger."

"Christ." Sherman had been a U.S. senator and Folger Secretary of the Treasury. You couldn't go much higher.

"Dan knew them all, didn't he?"

"Yes. He loved his friends. He was loyal. Allan thought a lot of him. Did you like Mr. Pinkerton?"

"For what? His penny-pinching? His big mouth? His boring talk?"

"As a man."

"Well, yeah. As a man, he was special. And I liked him despite all his faults."

"You have no faults?"

"Lots of 'em, ma'am, but none I can't live with."

"You're pretty smug. I'm surprised Allan would hire you. You seem—"

"Rough? Unschooled?"

"Yes. I'm sorry, I didn't mean to be offensive."

Raider got off the bed and stalked to a spot in front of her. He looked down into her eyes.

"What did you mean to be, ma'am?"

He was close enough to smell her faint musk under the perfume. Lilac scent couldn't hide a woman in season.

Her breasts rose and swelled against her bodice as she drew in a quick breath. Her tongue slid outside her mouth, licked wetness over her lips. She began to breathe rapidly, and her eyes grew cloudy.

"Mr. Raider, you...you don't know how it's been. I...since Len...I mean..."

"I know how it is," he said. "You come in heat and there

ain't no stud to service you. You start rolling around the bed and puttin' a pillow 'tween your legs, and the itchin' gets so danged bad you—"

"Stop it," she breathed, moving closer to him. "Don't torture me like this."

"Why, ma'am, I was just tellin' you how it was, you ain't havin' a man and all for two years. Unless you took in a boarder or strayed outside the fence."

"Never! I've been wearing black ever since—"

"Widow's weeds never stopped a bear from getting into the honey."

He took her roughly into his arms, bent her backwards. His kiss sizzled on her lips. He crushed her breasts into his chest, held her loins tightly against his crotch.

"Oh, yes," she said, when he broke the kiss. "Take me, Raider. That's what I want."

"Yes'm," he rasped, seeing the strawberry flush on her neck, listening to her panting. "I reckon that bear's gonna git him some honey."

CHAPTER TWO

Raider knew where all the fasteners were on Mary's dress. He peeled her out of her dress and tossed it over a chair. She stood there, shaking in her black panties, garters halfway up her calf. Her tiny brassiere barely held her ripe, full breasts. He knew where the fasteners were on that, too.

"Damned shame," he said, fondling one of her breasts. "Two years is too goddamned long."

She worked at his gunbelt with frantic fingers. Her eyes stared at the bulge in his crotch, glazed over with the frost of desire. She sagged as the heavy gunbelt loosened and weighted her hands. She dove at his trousers like a half-savage wanton, licking her lips.

Raider let her have her head. His trousers slid to his boot tops. She ripped his shorts down to his knees and gathered up his pouch and the hardening cock in cupped hands as if she was scooping up a package of raw meat.

"Hold on," he said. "We can't get far this way." He stepped back and found a chair. His boots clunked on the floor. He tossed his clothes in a heap as Mary stood there quivering like an aspen in a windstorm.

He got up, lifted her in his arms, carried her to the bed. She gazed up at him with a quizzical look. He smiled and reached down and drew her black panties down her legs. She shivered.

"Better spread 'em," he said, "else it'll be tough all around."

"Yes," she said, her eyes snapping back into focus.

Her black thatch glistened with a dewy sheen as he crawled

in beside her. His cock was rock-hard now, and she reached for it with trembling fingers.

She twined her fingers around his swollen shaft and squeezed the flesh in her palm. Raider explored the dark thatch between her legs; he plumbed a finger through her slit into the damp tunnel. Mary squirmed with pleasure and tightened her grip on his cock.

"I want it," she purred. "I want it inside me."

He nuzzled a breast, mouthed a nipple, worrying the nubbin between his lips. His finger drove up against the clit-tingle and tweaked it. Mary seemed to rise a good half foot off the bed as an electric shock jolted her body. Raider's finger slickened with a drench of warm fluid.

"I reckon," he said, withdrawing his finger. He crawled between her legs, mounted her.

Mary was ready. Her breasts rose and fell with her excited breathing. When his cock touched her labials, she jumped again, impaling the organ between pneumatic lips. Raider sank into the dank heat of her pussy, felt the folds of flesh give way.

"Oh, oh, oh!" she screamed, and her thighs shuddered.

Raider pushed on still deeper until her hot flesh swelled around his cock. A muscle in her groin twitched and tightened, locking him in.

"Fuck me, Raider," she wailed. "Fuck me good!"

"Yes'm."

He bored into her, stroking deep. Flesh smacked against flesh until the room was filled with the sound of their coupling. The bedsprings creaked and the bed swayed back and forth as Raider plumbed her cunt, humping her with a rhythm geared to her own frantic thrashings.

Mary was a good woman, he knew. She had just waited too long. Now she had let down all the barriers with a stranger. It happened all the time. He liked it that way. No strings. Just a man and a woman doing what came naturally. She would probably forget all about him by tomorrow. Or she might go out and find herself a good man who would come home at night and sit by the fire. The more you got, he'd heard, the more you wanted.

The man in the pearl-gray derby, its brim curled neatly all around, sucked thoughtfully on his cheroot as he read the framed page from the mint's rules and regulations for 1795. The document hung on the wall in Josiah Abernathy's office as if to remind those who entered of just how harsh life could be.

The time of work and Labour in the Mint, shall be understood by all employed therein, to be Eleven Hours in each Day—and shall from the 10th of November, begin at 6 o'clock in the morning and continue till 7 o'clock in the Evening allowing from 8 to 9 o'clock for Breakfast, and from 1 till 2 o'clock for Dinner.

He fished in his silk vest for a sulphur match. His finger curved to dig forth a lone match left there since morning. He was trying to cut down on his smoking, although he dearly loved the sweet Old Virginia cheroots. For a month now he had been rationing his matches, trying to keep from lighting the cigars. Each morning he put five matches in his vest pocket. Today he had ruined two of the matches through carelessness. One broke off when he tried to strike it, and the other's head had been faulty. So he was behind in his usual smoking, and his nerves twanged like a guitar string plucked when it was out of tune.

He struck the match on the corner of picture frame and shoved the cheroot into the flaring flame.

"Ah," he sighed as he drew smoke through the cigar.

Footsteps sounded down the hall.

Two people.

One would be that cute Miss Logan; the other would be Josiah Abernathy.

And they were coming in a hurry.

"Sir?" said Abernathy. "You have official business here?"

Abernathy swept into his office, followed by a worried Janet Logan.

"I do," said the man in the derby.

"Your card, sir."

A card was produced. The ink was barely dry.

"You're Henry Lee?"

"From Virginia, sir," lied Doc Weatherbee, his soft drawl perfectly mimicked. "And from the District."

Abernathy read the card.

Henry Lee

Inspector of the United States Mints

By Appointment of the President

"Yes. Very well." Abernathy thrummed the card in his hands, then walked to his desk. Miss Logan beamed with relief. Doc flashed her a smile and patted her fanny noiselessly. She blushed.

"Will there by anything else, Mr. Abernathy?" Her voice squeaked as she batted her eyelids at Weatherbee.

Abernathy didn't look up at her.

"No, that will be all, Miss Logan."

Doc winked at her before she turned and left the room. Miss Logan winked back and blushed once more.

"Does this—this inspection have anything to do with Secretary Windom?" asked Abernathy, clearly discomfited by the unexpected visit.

"It does. As you know, members of Congress debated on moving the Philadelphia mint to either New York or St. Louis. Through our efforts, the proposal was defeated, and we expect an appropriation soon to build another mint in Philadelphia, thus preserving our heritage."

"I'm so relieved to hear this, Mr. Lee. Do you know where the new mint will be located?"

"The mint will stand between Sixteenth and Seventeenth streets, its front on Spring Garden Street. The refineries will be in New York and here in Denver."

"Excellent choice. I disagreed thoroughly with Senator

Carter. I spent many pleasant years in the Philadelphia mint."

"So you did, Abernathy. Let's hope you have learned from the experience and from the Montana senator's appraisal."

Weatherbee suppressed the urge to gloat. He was certain that Abernathy was familiar with Montana Senator Thomas Carter's strong declaration in Congress after inspecting the Philadelphia mint:

> On the occasion of a recent visit to Philadelphia in connection with the annual Assay Commission, I was permitted to examine the various appliances and the rooms in which they were used at the mint, and I want to add my testimony to the fact that there does not exist on the continent today an intelligent and prudent businessman who would ask freeborn American citizens to spend their lives and perform their duties in the cold, damp, subterranean passages in which our fellow citizens are compelled to work in the mint at Philadelphia.

The bill passed after Carter's statement appeared in print, yet Weatherbee didn't foresee a third mint being finished until sometime after the turn of the century.

"Are you suggesting that perhaps Congress will approve a new mint for Denver?"

"That is highly likely," said Weatherbee. "In fact, my visit here is primarily fact-finding. My report goes to the highest office for evaluation."

Weatherbee enjoyed watching Abernathy's efforts to suppress his elation.

"Naturally," said Weatherbee, burying the seed even deeper, "Congress and the President are equally enthusiastic about your work here, Abernathy. The man who runs the new mint would have to be equally capable."

"Yes, ah, of course. If you're ready, Mr. Lee, perhaps we should begin. Is there any particular area of the mint you'd like to see first?"

"I'd like to start with the rolling machines, then go on to the planchet cutting room and perhaps see where the women adjust the planchets. That would be about all I'd have time for today." Weatherbee drew a gold Waterbury watch from the vest of his fancy cassimere worsted suit. He flipped open the case and glanced at it—but only to make the point with Abernathy that he was a busy and important man.

Actually, Doc Weatherbee was a Pinkerton agent, sent to work with Raider. He had already seen his erstwhile partner come and go from the mint and knew where he was staying. Since he preferred working under cover, he thought it best not to reveal his identity to Abernathy. Besides, he would probably learn a great deal more if Abernathy thought he was with the government. It didn't hurt to lie in such cases. In fact, it made the job that much sweeter.

They passed Janet Logan's office. Weatherbee winked at her as Abernathy swept along before him, doing his best to appear important and efficient. Miss Logan did not blush this time, but instead winked back. Doc, the eternal optimist, already knew what he would be doing later in the day. Let Raider have his fun with Brown's widow. The ripest peach was still on the tree.

The two men stopped briefly by the alloying room, where a man and a boy were ladling gold into molds. One furnace door was open, steaming with sulphurous fumes. The stench of sulphuric acid was very strong. The two workers wore aprons and gloves.

A box of ingots, sprinkled with powdered charcoal to prevent oxidation, lay on the floor near a wicker basket. The boy tended the furnace being used to melt the ingots. Each melt, or crucible, was done separately.

"They can handle four crucibles a day," said Abernathy.

The man with the ladle, which was actually a traingular-shaped cup held by a pair of tongs, dipped from the crucible, then poured the alloy slowly into a rectangular mold.

Weatherbee had been to the Philadelphia mint, fortunately, so he knew about much of the process of turning raw ore into coin of the realm. He noticed that the molds were bound in pairs, the unit made of three pieces, two U-shaped strips and a center piece making a partition between them. The bands holding the units together were made solid with a fixed screw.

The boy stood behind the man pouring the molten gold into the mold. As soon as the mold was filled, the man passed it to the boy, who dismantled it with hands heavily gloved, then threw the two red-hot ingots into a tank of clean water. Afterwards, Weatherbee knew, he would dip the ingots into a mild solution of sulphuric acid. Doc's nostrils were already irritated from the acid fumes.

"Those ingots," said Abernathy, "will be cut off on the topping machine, and the little fringe where the mold built up will be filed off."

"By hand," said Weatherbee. "And then the ingots will be stamped with their melt number and sent to the chief coiner."

Abernathy's brows arched only slightly.

Doc had passed the first test.

The rolling machine was a huge metal monster that bombarded the ears with the sound of thunder and whirring. Two men stood at either side of the wheeled demon, while a third stood at the bench were the long ingots were stacked. The harsh sound of steam could be heard above the whine of the large wheels turning the rollers.

Beneath the rollers a scale quivered as each ingot was fed through the maw of the machine.

There were four of the machines, each manned by three men in aprons. Abernathy walked to the first one. Every time the machine's big wheels turned, the room shook. Abernathy walked over to the operator and beckoned Doc to join him. The three men, all bearded and aproned, seemed to tolerate their superior but went about their work without showing any emotion. They ignored Doc completely.

"We've had steam since 1816," said Abernathy. "But we've done some improvements since then."

"I know," said Doc.

Abernathy frowned. He pointed to a throttle valve.

"Know what that does?" he asked.

Doc thought fast and tried to remember.

"Controls the speed during the rolling operation," he said.

"Right. Now we can overcome the irregularities in the ingots. Notice that the expensive gearing has been removed. That lets us adjust the difference between the rollers with that crank there, regulate it with a dial."

"I see."

Now Doc knew why there were four machines. Each was kept in a fixed, graduated series so that the ingot could pass freely through each. Abernathy stepped away from the big wheel to the draw bench, where a single man operated the complicated machinery.

"We've improved this, too," said Abernathy, pointing to four weights on two pulleys attached to the nearby wall. "Those automatically draw the carriage back to its starting position. See how they reduce the speed as the ingot approaches the iron stand?"

"Ingenious."

There were six planchet cutters at the rear of the rolling mills. These were also steam-driven and operated on the principle of an eccentric wheel. There were two wheels, one for each set of weights.

In another room men sat on stools, cutting planchets out of the flattened strips of metal. Doc and Abernathy watched them wordlessly for a few moments, then Abernathy knocked on a door. After a time it opened.

Women worked in the airless room. The scales were so sensitive that any draft would affect them. Doc looked at them and wondered how they could be so happy working under those conditions. Their pay, he knew, was no more than $1.15 a day. Yet they seemed contented, laughing and chatting among themselves. They seemed to scarcely glance at the planchets or scales, but seemed to be guided by touch alone.

A supervisor, who also weighed the coins, sat at a table

at one end of the room. Women sat facing each other at long tables set at right angles to the supervisors' station. Each woman had a set of scales and a metal bin in which to put the coins. They all had files. Doc stopped counting the number of women when he reached forty.

Abernathy rushed Doc through the rooms as the afternoon wore on. Doc learned that sometime in the 1860s the mint began adjusting only the gold coins and silver dollars. The overweight planchets were filed lightly on the edge and, after striking, hardly ever showed that an adjustment had been made. The other pieces, either slightly heavy or light, were coined separately, then mixed together, allowing each delivery to present a balanced weight.

Gold coins, except for the dollar, were counted by hand and weighed in the aggregate before being placed into bags. Gold dollars, silver, and minor coins were counted in a "counting board," a wooden tray partitioned by copper strips. The counters could work the board so well that twenty-five dollars in five-cent pieces were counted in less than a minute before being emptied through the front of a tray into a drawer.

The bags, Doc discovered, were heavy canvas, labeled "Denver Mint." He wondered if it was the practice to ship silver dollars in wooden crates. And with a hundred thousand dollars at stake, he wondered if there had been enough security the night of the robbery.

"Do you have a standard shipping procedure?" he asked Abernathy.

"Yes and no."

"Meaning?"

"We follow orders."

"Do you always agree with those orders?"

"To what are you referring, sir?"

"The night you were robbed of a hundred thousand pieces of silver."

Abernathy looked at Doc as if he were a bug that had come out of the woodwork. He pulled his pocket watch out and glanced at the time.

"Perhaps we'd best discuss this another time. Certainly not in front of the workers," he said curtly.

"No matter. Washington is still wondering if that was an inside job."

"Sir, how dare you!"

"Come off it, Abernathy. You signed the order that night. The silver is still missing."

"The investigation is continuing."

"I know that."

Abernathy ushered Doc from the counting room and back to his office. Miss Logan was bent over her desk, writing in a ledger, and did not see them.

Abernathy slammed the door.

"Have a chair, Mr. Lee," he said. Doc sat down.

Abernathy made an inverted V with his hands after he took his chair behind his desk.

"You've brought up a very sore subject around here, Lee. We've wondered, too, if it was an inside job. If you read the report, we only had one employee missing that night, a guard named Edward Grabowski. He had no prior knowledge of the shipment and was not very bright. All others were accounted for."

"Yes. Grabowski. He disappeared, didn't he?"

"No. He came in the next day, and he worked steadily until a month ago."

"Where is he now?"

"I believe his mother was dying and he went back east to be with her."

"Can you give me a description of him? A photograph?"

Abernathy was taken aback.

"No. I don't see that this concerns you. We have someone on the case," he said smugly.

"I'm interested in the security procedures, Abernathy."

"Harvard, isn't it?"

"Yes. You?"

"Princeton."

The two men seemed to square off as opposing forces. A knock at the door broke the tension in the room.

"Come in," said Abernathy.

Janet Logan came in with a stack of ledgers. She put them on her boss's desk. Doc stared at her fanny. She left, trying her best to avoid eye contact with Weatherbee.

"Will there be anything else, Mr. Lee? I really must get at these ledgers."

"She married?"

"Who?"

"Miss Logan there."

"Sir!" Abernathy rose from his chair, more than slightly discomfited. "That is not a proper question for a man with your responsibility."

Doc laughed and rose from his chair. He walked to the door, aligning his derby at a jaunty angle.

"She's got an extraordinary derriere," he said under his breath.

Abernathy wasn't sure of what the man had said. But when the door closed, he let out a sigh. That was the second time that day he'd heard a stranger refer to that particular part of Miss Logan's anatomy. Although the two phrases were different, they both meant the same thing. This was most curious.

"Henry Lee," he mused. "Now where have I heard that name before?"

A few seconds later he knew he'd been gulled.

Henry Lee had been governor of Virginia in 1792 when the long awaited "Act establishing a Mint and regulating the coins of the United States" had been enacted.

"The cad," he grumbled. "The utter cad!"

CHAPTER THREE

Mary's fingers traced the muscles in Raider's arms. A deep, satisfying shudder coursed through her body as she climaxed again. Her stomach fluttered with a thousand butterflies and her ears rang with the sounds of her own soft screams of pleasure.

Raider's muscles sleeked under sweat and his eyes glittered like light-shot gems. His sweat-oiled body moved against hers with powerful grace and a lithe, panther-like motion. Lamplight glowed in the room, spilling a coppery sheen over their naked bodies.

The bedsprings creaked with a lusty rhythm, and Mary's legs rocked in time with the thrusting of his loins.

His cock burrowed deep into her sheath and triggered sensations she had never known or had forgotten.

They had neither eaten nor slept, and the afternoon was gone; the night hovered outside the windows of the hotel room like a cloaking backdrop to their lovemaking.

"Raider," she sighed. "I don't know if I can give this up now."

"Don't."

"But it's so good. You're so good. I'm on fire. All over. And every time you slide across one part of me I tingle. Ummm. There. Oh, yes. Beautiful."

It was good. She was good. She gave him everything she had and then gave him more. The fire, yes. It was there. And the electric tingling. She had done things to him with her mouth, and he had done things to her. He had tried to break away, but every time she touched him, or looked at him, his cock turned to stone, rose up like an angry blind worm to plunge into that sweet mystery between her legs, past that dark patch of hair into the good hot honeyed juices of her sex.

She bucked and thrashed as he bore down, stepping up the tempo of his driving cock.

Then she froze solid as someone pounded on door.

"Jesus," said Raider. "Don't stop, Mary."

The knocking grew louder.

Raider kept humping, but there was no response. He was dead in the saddle. Finished—about a split-second before climax. The widow's eyes widened. He felt her hands on him, pushing him away.

"Just a goddamned minute!" he roared.

Mary, startled, jerked away from him instinctively. He spewed out of her, unsheathed.

"Please, I can't be found here like this..."

"Whoever it is, I'll send them away."

He climbed out of bed, drew on shorts and jeans, and hobbled to the door.

Even before he opened it, he knew who it was.

The air reeked of the unmistakable door of Old Virginia cheroots.

"Oh, shit!" said Raider. "It's that fuckin' Weatherbee."

"Huh?" said Mary, struggling nervously back into her clothes.

"What do you want?" Raider yelled through the door.

No answer.

Raider opened the door.

Weatherbee stood there grinning, his features obscured by wreaths of cigar smoke. Without waiting for an invitation, he strode into the room. His glance at Mary Brown could only be described as a knowing leer. Raider glared at him and balled up one fist.

"I hope I didn't interrupt anything important," said Doc.

"You didn't interrupt a damned thing. Now get out of here and let this lady get her clothes on."

"I'll just turn my back. This is isn't a social call. Not that it couldn't be if..."

"Doc, you say one more word and I'll break your jaw."

"Come now, Raider, is that any way to act in front of a lady?"

"I'm glad you called Mrs. Brown a lady."

Doc turned his back to Mary, who hurriedly slipped back into her clothes. Raider fumed. Doc smiled pleasantly and puffed on his cheroot.

"Actually," said Weatherbee, "it's most fortunate that you're here, Mrs. Brown. I wondered if you could shed some light on a certain individual."

"Come on, Doc, this ain't the time."

"I'll be happy to answer any questions if you're a Pinkerton man," she said.

"Agent," said Doc. "I am, but I'd appreciate your discretion. Safe to turn around?"

"Yes." Mary walked to the table and took a comb out of her purse. She began running it through her hair, slowly, methodically. "Won't you both sit down while I make myself presentable?"

Raider and Doc looked at each other. Raider shrugged. Doc pulled out a chair for Mary. Raider sat down. Doc stood, since there were no other chairs.

While Mary combed out her hair, Doc asked questions.

"Did you or your husband know a man named Grabowksi? Edward Grabowski?"

"Yes. Len knew him. He was a guard, I think."

"Was he supposed to ride with the shipment the night of the robbery?"

"I . . . I don't know. Len was mad about something. Having to work so late, I think."

"Who's Grabowski?" asked Raider.

Doc pulled a small notebook out of his inside coat pocket and drew a pencil from his vest.

"Maybe nobody," said Doc. "Maybe one of those in on the robbery. Can you describe him for me, Mrs. Brown?"

"Grabowski? Big man. Not tall. Wide. Muscles. Lots of muscles. I don't remember him all that well. I used to see him with a shotgun when there was a shipment from the mint."

"Ever see him talk to anyone before the robbery?"

"I don't understand what you mean."

"Strangers. Look like he was whispering."

"No. I hardly went to the places·he frequented."

"Oh? Like where?"

"The Nugget on Larimer. The Curtis Street Saloon. A lot of the men workers go there on Saturday nights. So Leonard told me."

Doc wrote it all down. Mary continued combing out her hair.

"How do you know so damned much, Doc? I just got here this morning."

"May we see you home, Mrs. Brown," said Weatherbee politely. "Mr. Raider and I have some urgent business."

"No. It would be better if you did not. Will I see you again, Raider? Soon?"

Raider swallowed hard.

Doc leered.

"Yes'm. Real soon."

"Good night, then. I hope you and Mr. . . . Doc Weatherbee can solve this case. Remember what I told you, Raider."

"Uh huh."

The door closed quietly. Raider balled up his fist again.

"What did she tell you, Raider?"

"That woman wants revenge, Doc. No prisoners."

"I can understand why. Her husband died hard."

"Two years ago. Now how in hell do you know so goddamned much about this case? I just got orders from Wagner a week ago in Cheyenne."

"Get your clothes on, Raider. We have a lot to do. And, to answer your question, I've been working on this case off and on for four months, and I've been in Denver for two weeks."

Raider pulled on his boots and slid into his shirt. Both were wrinkled.

"You been to the mint?"

"Today," said Doc.

"See Abernathy?"

"I saw him."

"What do you make of him?"

"I think your opinion would be more colorful, Raider."

"He's an asshole. I don't think he knows anything about the robbery. He's too...too..."

"Fastidious?"

"I guess. Slowtidious'd be more like it."

"I'd like to see the silver dollars he gave you."

"You know about them? He tell you?"

"He doesn't know who I am. But Wagner set this operation up. He said you'd be given some samples of the coins."

"I got 'em." Raider dug them out of his trouser pockets.

Doc took them and began to examine them. He looked at the edges very carefully; he held them up to the light. Raider finished dressing, stuck his Stetson on his head, and brushed out his mustache. Doc put the coins on the table. Raider walked over, curious.

"What're you doing?" he asked.

Doc reached into his coat pocket and pulled out two strips of felt. Chunks of round silver were affixed to the sticky surface. He shook them and they unfolded, dangling like a pair of Chinese banners. The silver glinted in the lights.

"What you see here, Raider, are unstruck coins from the Denver mint."

"So?"

"So, they have an exact silver content. Measurable. And they have been filed by pretty ladies in drab dresses who toil long hours for meager stipends."

"Bring it down to gut level, Doc."

"Observe," said the dapper, glib-tongued Weatherbee, as he magically produced a set of coins from another pocket. These were wrapped in felt as well, but without the sticky substance. The coins clattered on the table, spun crazily, and came to rest next to the others.

"Cartwheels. Silver dollars."

"Look closely, my friend."

Raider picked up one of the blanks, prying it loose from the felt strip.

"Now, gander the ones I just dropped on the table."

The tall man picked one up and held it next to the blank. He read the legends and looked at the female figure seated upon bales of cotton (a sheaf of wheat in the rear), holding in her right hand, which is extended toward the open sea, an olive branch. The date of coinage read 1871. There were thirteen stars surrounding the figure and the motto "In God We Trust" at the base of the device. This was the obverse side. The reverse side carried the figure of an eagle, and on a scroll in the open field above, "E Pluribus Unum," and above that the inscription "United States of America." Below the eagle were the inscriptions "420 grains, 900 fine," and "trade dollar" and a scroll bearing the motto "In God We Trust." Both sides were in relief. They looked genuine.

"Trade dollars," said Raider.

Doc laughed and slapped Raider on the shoulder. He had to reach up to do it.

"You bet your Middleton boots they're trade dollars."

"I don't get it. Are you saying these are the stolen cartwheels?"

"Umm. Maybe. We'll do some tests to find out. On a strong hunch, I'd say yes. See what they say?"

"United States of America, that eee pluriboos yunum whatchamacallit."

"E Pluribus Unum. Out of many, one. Latin. And maybe not so inappropriate for these well-struck beauties. What else do you see there?"

And, very small, on either side of the "trade dollar" legend, were the words "Pecos" and "Mint."

"'Pecos Mint.' Never heard of it."

"We know this much. These are privately minted. These 'Pecos dollars' have been turning up in St. Louis, Chicago, New York, Kansas City, and New Orleans. The Secretary of the Treasury is having a fit. That pattern you see was struck in 1871 using a leftover obverse die of J. B. Longacre. In '72, Barber copied the Longacre design and added a couple of trade dollar reverses, one with a wreath device, the other with a standing eagle."

"You stole these from the mint today?"

"I did."

"How?"

"Dropped those felt strips into the bin and made sure they stuck to the coins. Sleight of hand, a little luck, distraction."

"A magician's tricks."

"If you wish. It was necessary. Because the Secretary thinks that robbery was an inside job, it's important we don't put all our cards on the table when we deal with Abernathy. Or Mrs. Brown, for that matter."

"Doc, you've lost me. I thought Mary Brown started this investigation. She's a friend of Bill Pinkerton's."

"She was part of the investigation from the night of the robbery. Everyone, even Abernathy, was a suspect. The trail was cold from the start. Until these trade dollars started showing up. Pinkerton was glad to tell Mrs. Brown he would put us on the case, but he was already on it. In fact in about twenty minutes we're to meet the operative who's been on it since the beginning. Lucas Skye is over at the Cherry Creek Saloon on Larimer, or should be. I think he might have information on where these Pecos dollars are coming from."

"Luke Skye? Here? Hell, he's heavy caliber. His pistol butt's got more notches on it than a bulldog's ear. Damn it, Doc, why in hell was I kept in the dark about all this?"

"You know the Pinkertons. Like the Lord and Congress, they move in mysterious ways."

CHAPTER FOUR

Raider looked at the Studebaker with contempt. His eyes swept to the mule standing hipshot in its traces.

"Hell, Doc, we can walk to Larimer Street."

"Might need the wagon. Climb up."

"I see you still have that flea-bitten, broken-down nag."

"Judith's not a nag, and, while she may not understand your words, she knows your tone. Don't offend her."

"Shit," said Raider, climbing into the Studebaker. The wagon was gaudy with legend, proclaiming Doc Weatherbee's "miracle cures" and such. The lettering on the sides was faded but visible. Doc climbed up, incongruous in his fancy garb against the seedy appearance of the wagon. Still, he kept it up, mechanically, and there were secret compartments that held various devices that only Doc knew how to use. Under the floor, for instance, a pull-up compartment housed his telegraph key and gravity batteries, rolls of wire, tools, etc. In another place, Raider knew, Doc kept his Premo Sr. camera, plates, chemicals, and various attachments.

Doc clucked to the mule, and the wagon moved away from the hotel, headed toward Larimer Street.

What bothered Raider was that Doc knew more about this case than he himself did, and what information he had gotten had only left him confused. All this talk about coins, engravers, weights, and the Pecos mint made him wonder if they'd ever find the thieves. The tracks not only seemed to be well covered, but they were clouded behind a lot of technical jargon that made the unknown faces of the criminals even more shadowy. Raider couldn't put his finger on anything tangible. He couldn't put his hands around anyone's neck.

"I finally figured out your secret, Raider," said Doc, letting Judith have her head. The mule stepped along at a leisurely pace, her hoofbeats oddly soothing in the relative quiet of evening.

"What secret's that?"

"With the women."

"Yeah?"

"You and that widow Brown. Heard the way you talked to her. Putting on that corncake Kentucky farmboy dialect before you put the boots to her."

"Doc, you're one son of a bitch. And it's not Kentucky. It's Arkansas."

"Same thing. The Arkies all came out from Kentucky. Dumb bunch."

Raider knew Doc was goading him. He wondered why. Did he want his temper up when they saw Skye? Or found out what the operative had to say?

"You make a habit of listening at a man's door?"

"Didn't want to break in on you, friend."

"The hell you say. You've done it often enough before. And don't call me 'friend.' I'd sooner be with the Wild Bunch up in the Hole in the Wall than work an assignment with you."

Doc turned Judith onto Larimer.

The street was in full swing, saloons blaring with light, raucous with laughter, the clink of glasses, the sad tinkle of a tinny piano, the plaintive strains of a Mexican guitar crying out the notes of a *son huasteco*. Horses and mules stood at hitch rings, and men weaved from one saloon to another like sailors on shore leave.

Named after William Larimer, ex-major general of the Pennsylvania Militia, engineer, banker, merchant, freighter, legislator, and founder of La Platte City, Nebraska, the street was broad and open. It was ironic that it boasted so many saloons. Larimer had been a teetotaler.

Doc pulled the wagon up in front of the Cherry Creek

Saloon and set the brake. Raider climbed down and looked around as Doc secured the rig. He hadn't seen Luke Skye in a long while, and that had been a brief meeting when both had court dates to testify in separate cases. But he knew if Luke was on the case there was a lot more muscle behind the investigation than he had suspected.

"What do you expect to get out of Skye?" Raider asked Doc as they touched boots to the boardwalk.

"He's been working on this almost two years; he thinks he has something for us."

"Why meet here?"

Doc shrugged.

Raider didn't like it. Luke was even more undercover than they were. This was a public place. A rough public place.

The saloon was crammed with bleary-eyed miners, tramps, boom-town scum. Doc stood out like a sore thumb in his derby and cassimere suit.

"About half these men are on the dole," said Raider.

"Watch your moneybelt."

Doc's eyes flickered as he scanned the room looking for Lucas Skye.

"Over there," said Raider, tilting his head toward a far corner. The two men stalked past crowded tables, leaving skid marks in sawdust as they made their way to Skye's table. A waiter with a grimy apron dodged them, deftly balancing a tray full of bottles and glasses. Smoke hung hazy in the room, blue in the lantern light. The smell of coal oil mingled with the reek of whiskey, beer, brandy, and cigar and cigarette fumes.

"Skye," said Doc, looking not at him but at the derelict seated next to him.

"Take chairs, boys," said the Pinkerton.

Luke was short and wiry, with a swooping handlebar mustache. His clothes fitted him well. A duster failed to conceal the twin Colts he wore high on his belt. He had on a wide-brimmed Stetson, tweed suit, Mexican-made boots. His face was leathered from the sun and wind; his eyes, close-set, were a pale blue, frosty clear. A pail of beer sat on the table, the rim crawling with flies.

Doc and Raider sat down.

"What do we have here?" asked Doc.

"Howdy, Raider. Long time. Doc, you look fit."

Raider nodded a greeting and licked his lips.

Skye waved to a waiter.

"Have yourselves a drink on the company," he said.

"We don't have—"

"Shut up, Doc," said Raider quietly. "The man's buying us a drink."

Doc continued to look at the man next to Skye. But he held his tongue.

The derelict shrank back in his filthy clothes; looking at them with rheumy eyes. He reached for the beer pail and pulled it toward him. He lifted it with shaky hands and slopped beer into his thick glass. Skye drew in a breath. There was no glass in front of him.

"This here's Lemuel Parsons Naylor," said Luke. "Lem was what you might call an eyewitness."

"To what?" asked Doc cynically.

Raider's mustache twitched as he looked at the derelict with renewed interest.

"I seen 'em," said Naylor. His voice squeaked in a high-pitched rasp. His beard was bushy, threaded with dried food remnants. "Seen 'em shoot those men down."

"Better than that," said Luke. "He talked to Leonard Brown before anyone else did."

The waiter came over and stood there impatiently.

"Bring these boys what they want," drawled Luke. "And I'll have a taste of *aguardiente* to boot."

"Whiskey," said Raider quickly.

"Rye," said Doc.

"It's all the same here," said Luke.

"Rye," said Doc again, pulling out a cheroot. He seemed to pull away from Naylor as if to avoid smelling the man.

The waiter drifted away.

"You talked to Brown?" asked Doc.

"Plain as ever."

"Did he tell you anything? Did he know any of the robbers?"

"Told me a short man shot him."

"That all?"

"Nope." Naylor downed the beer in his glass. Foam clung to his beard. He made no move to wipe any of it away. Doc figured his beard must weigh twenty pounds with all the detritus clinging to it.

Luke smiled.

"Go on, Lem, tell them what you told me."

Lem told them. He had been sleeping in an alley when he heard the commotion. He woke up and came upon the robbery just before the bandits rode off. He saw the final blasts of the shotgun and watched the other wagon pull away in the darkness. When he heard moans, he ventured up to the freight wagon and saw that Brown was still alive. Brown spoke to him. It was difficult to understand everything he said.

"Try to remember," said Doc wryly.

"Well, he told me about the men and said one of 'em was real slender and not a man."

"Huh?" said Raider. "Go by that again."

"It's what he said. He called one 'Shorty,' another 'Baldy.' Like he knew 'em."

The Pinkertons exchanged glances.

"That isn't the most important thing, though," said Luke. "Lem here, bless his drunken soul, recognized the wagon that the thieves used to haul off the silver dollars."

"'At's right," said Lem. "It was a hearse. And I used to sweep out at the undertaker's what owned it."

Doc's eyes glittered with interest. Raider turned to take the bottle and glass from the waiter before he could lower his tray. Luke watched the waiter set down a bottle of brandy and another of rye and two more glasses.

Lem reached out and rattled the empty pail.

"More beer," said Luke.

"Whiskey," said Lem.

"No whiskey yet, Lemuel. You just tell us more about that hearse."

"Yessir, it belonged to Mr. Welch. Roger Welch. Welch's Undertaking Parlor over on Gilpin."

Raider drank a finger of whiskey neat and straight.

Luke poured Doc's glass, then his own, before pushing his chair back so he could lean against the wall.

"Did you follow up on this, Luke?" asked Doc.

"I saw Welch. He claimed Lem here was a bald-faced liar."

"Not me," said Lem, rising up to see if the waiter was coming with a fresh pail of warm beer. "That was his hearse. I'd recognize it anywhere. Friend of mine rode in it once."

Raider asked the next question.

"You look at the hearse, Luke?"

"He has three of them. The one Lem described is still there. I went over it the other night. After two years, there wasn't much. Just this, stuck down between the padded floorboards."

Skye fished out a silver dollar, put it edgewise on the table, and spun it like a top. Raider snatched it up and looked at it closely.

"Matches the pair I've got," he told Doc.

"Let me see."

Doc caught the coin as Raider flipped it to him.

"Interesting, isn't it?" asked Skye.

"Most," said Doc. "It's a match, all right. So you've got that much. You figure Welch was in on it."

"He's scared. So was Lemuel here until I pointed out that he could be named as an accessory after the fact if he didn't tell me all he knew. There's more. And a lot of it is just sky-blue thinking on my part. Ever hear of a man named Baron Walter von Richthofen?"

Raider shook his head.

Doc nodded. "Prussian aristocrat," he said. "Came to Denver in the late seventies. Threw a lot of money around, said he was going to put Denver on the map. He was involved in a real-estate deal south of town. It didn't work.

Too far out. He put in a beer garden, said he was going to run a railroad spur to his development. Tried to lure the rich boys into settling there."

"Well, he's built a new suberg east of town, calls it Montclair," said Skye.

"Suburb," said Doc.

"Built hisself a castle," said Lemuel. "I been in it."

Luke smiled.

Doc's eyebrows lifted.

Raider poured another drink.

No one spoke for several seconds. Naylor licked his lips when he saw the waiter coming with his beer. The buzz of conversation rose up around them and then fell off suddenly.

The waiter dumped the pail on the table. Luke handed him coin and waved him away. Naylor poured beer into his glass. He didn't spill very much of it. He drank greedily. The three men watched it dribble down his bearded chin and soak into his begrimed shirt.

"Interesting thing," said Skye. "The baron hired our friend Lem here shortly after the robbery. Lem told Welch that someone had used his hearse."

"Welch was awful mad," said Lem. "Called me a bald-faced liar. But the day after the robbery, that hearse wasn't at the parlor barn. It was out at the baron's. I heard Mr. Welch send someone to fetch it."

"Welch know you heard that?" asked Raider.

"Nope. But I told him I was sure that the robbers used that hearse. Didn't know what they took until someone read me the story in the *Rocky Mountain News*. Made my skin crawl."

"You've got something here, Luke," said Doc. "Any ideas? The blue-sky ones will do."

"Yesterday the baron had a pair of visitors. I went out there in one of those fancy carriages he uses to haul pro-spective buyers to his suburb. Here comes the baron riding alongside, a pack of wolfhounds racing behind him. He meets a pair on horseback in front of his castle. One of them looked like a wrestler or a prizefighter. He wore no hat, and his head was clean as a baby's butt."

"And the other?" asked Doc quietly.

"The other was—"

Skye's eyebrows arched in surprise. His eyes widened. Whatever he had been about to say was drowned out in the explosion.

Fire and lead spewed from the snouts of a double-barreled shotgun. White smoke billowed behind the deafening thunder of ignited powder. Double-ought buckshot ripped through Luke's flesh. Naylor caught the lead from the second blast. Both shots were at close range, just over the heads of Doc and Raider.

Blood spouted from a dozen wounds as Skye shot backwards in his chair, impelled by the blast. Naylor crumpled, his neck blown half away; he sagged to the floor.

Raider slammed Doc sideways, whirled, tried to see through the smoke. His right hand clawed for his pistol.

Men yelled and dove for cover.

Doc, off-balance, tried to keep his chair from teetering over. Boots thudded on the floor, pounded on sawdust.

"He's getting away!" yelled Doc.

Raider's pistol filled his hand, but smoke stung his eyes and blurred his vision. He heard the running man but couldn't see well enough to shoot. He cursed under his breath and stood up.

The footsteps died away.

Doc managed to right his chair. He jerked his Diamondback .38 from its concealed holster and stood up next to Raider.

Behind them, Naylor gagged on blood.

Skye lay silent as death.

Men began shouting and talking.

Then they ran, clogging the doorway, blocking Raider and Doc from pursuit of the assassin.

"Anyone see the man with the shotgun?" Doc shouted. "Who was he?"

The smoke cleared; the room emptied.

The bartender and a waiter stared at the two Pinkertons

and then turned their faces away.

"Well?" asked Raider. "Did you two see the bastard?"

The two men shook their heads.

"Professional," said Doc, looking at Skye's blood-spattered face.

"Very," said Raider.

CHAPTER FIVE

Julius Goldberg looked over the tops of his pince-nez at the two men standing on the other side of the counter. He was a short, muscular man with a bald pate framed by graying frizzled hair that seemed to corkscrew in all directions. His small, aquiline nose looked sharp enough to cut meat and contrasted with his full, sensuous lips.

"You want me to do what, gentlemen?" he asked.

"Run a quick, private assay," said Doc. "Now and with no witnesses."

Raider towered over Doc's shoulder, over the diminutive assayer, sole proprietor of Goldberg's Smelting and Assay Service near 19th and Arapahoe.

"I've got a shop full of bullion, ingots, nuggets, foreign coins, jewelry, and plate that was here longer than you, and it's all quick and private."

Doc patted the lapel of his freshly brushed coat as if removing something distasteful that had not been there until he entered Goldberg's shop.

"Let me put it this way, Goldberg. You'll be doing your government a service and will be paid handsomely in the bargain."

"What's the government ever done for Julius Goldberg? Nothing, that's what. Biggest thieves in this country sit there in Washington and tell the rest of us how much we have to pay to be good citizens."

"He's got you there, Doc," said Raider, no trace of a smile on his lips. His sleek mustache gleamed raven-black in the morning sunlight streaming through the window.

"Raider, keep your trap shut."

44

"Hey, wait a minute. You Pinkertons?"

"He is," said Doc, pointing to Raider. "I'm—"

Goldberg stuck out his hand. "Never mind, I want to shake your paw, mister. Janet Logan was by yesterday, told me how you pulled one over on old Abernathy. Said he was fit to be tied. Described you to a T. You gulled him. You gulled him good."

Weatherbee coughed, pretended embarrassment. "What about this assay?"

"Be glad to, if it means more trouble for Abernathy. He thinks he's God up there in the mint. Hell, I taught all his damned assayers and smelters everything they know. You men come on back and we'll weigh you out, see what you got."

Raider smiled at Doc, who shot him a glance of annoyance in return.

Goldberg lifted a panel on the counter and let the Pinkertons inside his office. He led them through a door into a storeroom piled high with tagged silver and gold items, everything from bags of ore to fine plate. Raider let out a low whistle.

"It looks like a pawnbroker's," he said.

Doc gave him a wincing look.

Goldberg ignored the remark. He opened another door that led down a passageway to a huge warehouse-like building. The passageway was strewn with graying bones from various animals.

"Bone alley," said Goldberg cryptically. Inside the large room, tables were set in orderly fashion, and at the far end the smelting furnaces burned hot, sending smoke up a large earthen and brick chimney that was common to them all.

"Over here," said the assayer, pointing to a corner table set off by itself. Skylights in the ceiling poured columns of buttery luminescence into the huge room. Goldberg's table seemed to have the best light of all.

"Now, then, let's see what you got," he said, putting on a little cap that covered his bald pate but allowed patches of hair to stick out the sides.

Doc laid out the coins in sequence, but he explained none of his theories to Goldberg. He set out one of the coins given Raider by Abernathy; the blanks he had purloined at the Denver mint; a Pecos dollar; and the silver dollar they had gotten from Lucas Skye before he had been murdered.

The Pinkerton operatives watched as Julius filled out some form sheets with the stub of a charcoal pencil which he continually whittled to a fine point with the worn blade of a Barlow pocketknife. He spoke almost continually as he worked, as if to himself, but there was obvious pride in his tone. He was a craftsman. With his sleeves rolled up on delicate, almost hairless arms, he appeared oddly feminine with his small hands and sensitive fingers. He looked, thought Doc, like a washerwoman about to hand-scrub fine silk lingerie.

"We get a lot of metal in here," said Goldberg, "in every form you can imagine. But whatever the form, it almost always contains an alloy of other metals, and sometimes traces of nonmetallic substances. So to find out what it's made of, we have to refine it, just as if it was raw ore. If you had come in here as regular customers, we'd have weighed it out and given you a receipt by the weight, not the value."

Goldberg weighed the coins and blanks separately and together. He made notations on his tally sheet.

"Usually," he said, "we do not assay foreign coins, or coins of well-established character, since their fineness is marked on the face. But these are not so marked. So I'll take a sample from each—what we call a 'test'—and determine the character of each coin."

The assayer took a small knife and scraped a small piece from each coin. He trimmed each "test" to a prescribed weight, carefully weighing it until the scales balanced to 12 grains. He then placed each test within a cone of thin lead sheets. He pressed each cone into a ball and put them in separate bone-ash cupels. These were small dishes filled with paste made from the ashes of animal bones.

"Now we know why that hallway is known as 'bone alley,'" said Doc.

Raider, fascinated with Goldberg's intensity as he worked, merely nodded. The room was hot, and he was sweating, but the assayer appeared impervious to the heat.

The Pinkertons followed Julius to the assay furnace and watched as he put the cupel under a tunnel-shaped wrought-iron muffle within. He closed the door of the furnace carefully.

"That's a charcoal fire," he said. "I can watch the progress of cupellation through the small hole in the door of the furnace. Go ahead, take a look."

Doc and Raider both peered through the opening. Both were mystified.

Goldberg laughed and shoved them aside so he could monitor the process.

"As that cupel becomes red hot," he said, his voice rebounding off the furnace door, "the base metals oxidize rapidly. They'll begin to trickle out, and the porous cupel will absorb them. That lead covering I put over the test serves two purposes. First, it forms a highly liquid oxide which washes away the oxides of the other base metals. Second, it keeps a portion of the silver from volatilizing from the direct contact of the heat."

"If you say so," said Raider.

"He means it won't fly all over the place," Doc explained.

When the cupellation was finished, Goldberg weighed the small bead that was left of the test.

"Now we know the approximate loss of the base metals and can determine the fineness of the silver. There is some error possible, so we proof the test piece by cupelling a known standard piece at the same time. That furnace has to be just right, and now we know it is, so I'll proof the rest of the tests."

Goldberg called an assistant over, and the cupellation went rapidly in the 4,000-degree-Fahrenheit furnace.

The refining took most of the day. Neither Goldberg nor

the Pinkertons broke for lunch. As the light began to fade in the factory, Goldberg made his final notations.

He looked up at the operatives and grunted. He pulled a heavy timepiece from his watch pocket and glanced at the hands.

"Almost time for Janet Logan to arrive," he said.

"She comes here every day?" asked Doc.

"Sure does. Her last stop before going home to Nettie Wheeler's boardinghouse over on Broadway. Drops off small samples Abernathy sends over to check on his assayers and picks up my reports to take back the next day. In this case, Monday. And she gives me the news of Abernathy's latest foibles."

"You don't think much of him, do you?" asked Raider.

"He's competent. Pompous as a nut-heavy bull in a herd of steers. Keeps too firm a hand on everyone who works there, and that's why he's unsure of himself. You got that many employees, you can't watch 'em all. Come on up to the office and we'll have some tea, talk about your assay."

The furnaces seemed to bellow and heave as the workers began shutting them down. The skylights began to darken as the afternoon shadows smudged the surrounding buildings.

On the way to the office, Doc whispered instructions to Raider.

"You'd better check out Welch tonight," he said.

"What're you going to do?"

"I have some checking of my own to do. See you tomorrow. On Sunday, we'll pay the baron a visit at his castle."

"Just like that?"

"We'll be his guests," said Doc.

Goldberg's office was a clutter of papers, documents, scales, weights, charts, and assorted blobs of metal. His desktop was almost invisible. He brewed his tea in a crucible over a hot fire in a potbellied stove. He poured tea into cracked, stained cups. Open windows helped cool the room.

"Now," he said, leaning back in a large chair, "what do you want to know?"

"Everything," said Doc. "Whether or not the Pecos dollar is the same weight and fineness of the blanks and the Denver mint coin."

"Don't get too technical," said Raider defensively.

"All right," said Julius. "The coin minted here in Denver is four hundred and a half grains. So are the blanks. And so is the Pecos dollar. Copper content assays the same. I'd say the Pecos dollar was coined with obsolete machinery. Two men could do it, though, with a screw coining press. The metal is not dark, so whoever did it knew his business."

"Who might such a man be?" asked Doc.

"Someone who has worked in a mint, who knows every single operation."

Doc looked at Raider sharply.

"Know anyone like that?" asked Raider casually.

"Albert Metz."

Doc's eyebrows elevated.

The names were beginning to count up. Grabowski, Metz. Muscle and brains. But that wasn't enough. Doc knew it wasn't. There were five people involved in the actual robbery and murder. Metz was probably not in on that. He'd have Wagner check on him, see if he could be located. He also wanted to know if Metz, or anyone, had bought any used equipment from the U.S. Mint or any private minting firms. There was another name or two to check out as well. The undertaker, Welch, and Baron von Richthofen. Raider could give Welch a going-over this evening, and they could both give the baron a visit on Sunday.

As for himself, Doc had other plans for the evening.

She walked in the door right at that very moment.

"Hello, Mr. Goldberg," said Janet Logan. And, "Oh!" when she saw Raider and Doc.

Doc rose to his feet and bowed. Janet flushed. Raider watched them with narrowed eyes. Both men removed their hats.

"What have you got for me, Janet?" asked Goldberg.

She laid down a sheaf of papers and a small wooden box.

"Mr. Abernathy was called away suddenly. To the District of Columbia. He left in a hurry, and he was angry."

"Know what it was about?" asked Doc, offering her his chair.

"He didn't say, but I gathered it was urgent."

"Did he ask for anything special to take with him?"

"Why, yes, he did. Some personnel files. Miss Hastings got them for him."

"Miss Hastings?" asked Raider. Doc never batted an eye. He knew a great deal about Miss Hastings, indeed, about Abernathy's entire staff, and especially about Miss Logan.

"A clerk. He... he sent me out of the room while he gave the order."

Doc said nothing, but he could see Wagner behind this. Abernathy apparently had plenty to answer for. His guess would be that his message to Wagner last night, mentioning Grabowski, had triggered this new probe. A little late in the day.

Janet and Goldberg chatted briefly. Raider fiddled with his mustache, lost in thought. Doc watched her intently. He already knew where she lived. He knew a great deal more, too. She was not a virgin. Until two weeks ago, she had been meeting a printer's devil after work on Saturdays, spending the late-afternoon hours with him in his room. The youth, one Albert Newcomb, was down with the pox and Janet would not be seeing him. She was extremely nervous and frustrated and had missed church the past two Sundays in a row. He knew also that her father, an itinerant preacher, a widower, was due back in Denver on Monday and would demand that she accompany him to Cheyenne, where he was to be given his own church and flock. Janet's mail had told him much, and her fellow boarders had told him even more. He knew she didn't want to leave either Denver or Albert. Especially since her father had learned of her trifles and had plans for her to train for the ministry under his tutelage. Branfield Logan was a stern parent who was not above planting a spy in the boardinghouse who reported every indiscretion, real or imagined, to Logan.

Doc thought he had a solution that would satisfy her father and keep Janet working at the mint. He needed her there a while longer. She was the most vulnerable of those employees close to Abernathy. Miss Willa Hastings, an old crone, was fiercely loyal to her superior and would not divulge one iota of his business. Doc knew. He had tried, indirectly, and her replies had led him to Janet Logan. Nor was Albert her only swain. Miss Logan was an extremely precocious young lady and as fickle as a she-pup in heat.

He was jarred loose from his reverie by Raider's voice interrupting the conversation between Janet and Goldberg.

"How long ago did Abernathy get that message?" he asked Janet.

"Why, it was late this afternoon, just before I left work. In fact, Mr. Abernathy departed only a few minutes before I did."

"How was that message delivered?"

"By messenger."

"What're you getting at, Raider?" asked Doc.

"Maybe nothing." Raider glanced at the window; it was darkening fast now outside. "What time was he to catch the train east?"

"I...I don't know. He was in a terrible hurry."

Raider got to his feet. Everyone stared at him. He set his hat square on his head.

"Where are you going?" Doc asked as Raider strode to the door without so much as a by-your-leave.

"Let you know later. No time."

And then he was gone.

"I wonder what that was all about?" asked Janet.

"So do I, my dear," said Doc.

He knew he had missed something. Raider had caught it.

But what?

CHAPTER SIX

Raider knew damned well that Abernathy was being set up. He just hoped he would be on time to avoid disaster. Darkness was settling into the Denver streets when he caught a horse-drawn taxi going to the Denver Pacific railroad station. Kansas Pacific also had a line running to Cheyenne, but a quick inquiry at the Windsor, where he caught the hansom, revealed that the D.P. had a train leaving at 8:00 P.M.

"Hurry it up," said Raider to the driver.

"Keep your pants on, mister."

Anyone could send a telegram. Raider was sure that the one sent to Abernathy was bogus. There was no good reason for such a request. Wagner would have let him or Doc know if Washington was sending for Abernathy. A check at his hotel after he left the assay office had revealed no such message from the Pinkerton office. Doc had accepted Janet Logan's account without question, but the moment he had learned of this development, he knew that something was amiss. It just didn't ring right. Yet Abernathy had swallowed it.

When the Logan woman had mentioned the personnel files, that had clinched it. Someone wanted those files and wanted Abernathy out of the way at the same time.

Damn Doc, anyway. He should have tumbled to it. He had his eyes stuck on Janet Logan and had missed it.

The cab rumbled into the yards and pulled up to the station.

"Wait for me," said Raider, handing the driver a bill.

"How long?"

"Until I get back."

The cabbie's reply was drowned in the blast of a train whistle, the dragon-like hiss of steam.

A locomotive pulling a string of freight and passenger cars moved toward the depot.

Raider started to run.

Passengers began streaming out of the station building, lining up along the tracks. Raider looked for Abernathy among them but did not see him. He lengthened his strides as the train picked up speed.

Abernathy emerged from the depot alone.

He carred a carpetbag, a small satchel tucked under his arm.

Raider was still too far away to yell. The noise of the train would have drowned him out anyway.

Then the thing that he had dreaded happened.

A short man broke from the crowd and approached Abernathy. He wore a loose duster, a derby hat. One hand was shoved inside the duster, the other waved at the mint director.

To Raider's chagrin, Abernathy began following the short man, around the opposite end of the building.

Raider saw why.

The snout of a rifle, or shotgun, slipped out from under the shorty's duster.

"Shit," said Raider, drawing his pistol.

His side started to ache as he exerted extra effort to run faster. His lungs began to burn.

He cocked the pistol automatically, a reflex, and knew he would be too late. Abernathy and the small man disappeared around the corner of the building. Passengers began boarding the train, which had grated to a stop with a screech of steel sliding along steel. The locomotive jetted out clouds of steam and rumbled with the fire in its belly-box. The cars shivered as they jolted to a halt; they clattered like a stack of giant metallic dominoes falling together in series.

Moments seemed to stretch into hours as the two men disappeared from view. The last passenger stood on the running board of the train when a blast of gunfire boomed over the noise of the train.

Raider reached the boardwalk border of the station house and increased his stride.

Another blast rocked him as he rounded the corner.

Abernathy was on the ground, half sitting, his belly shot away. Blood spattered his shirt and vest.

Gone were his satchel and carpetbag.

Raider heard footsteps runnning away and whirled in their direction. People on the train peered through the windows trying to see what had happened.

Abernathy toppled over, his throat rattling with blood clogging his air passage. Raider stopped briefly to see if there was anything he could do for the man. The director's eyes clouded over with the frost of death. His throat made one last gurgle. His chest stopped moving.

Raider began running after the retreating footsteps. Away from the lights of the station it was hard to see. The train hooted again, drowning out the sounds of his quarry. His eyes strained at the darkness; his nerves twanged at every moving shadow.

He saw him then, the short man, sneaking behind the massive hulk of a freight car on a side track. The man was struggling to carry the stolen objects, but he moved fast nevertheless. Raider raised his pistol for a shot. The short man paused and looked back.

Raider took aim and squeezed the trigger.

The Remington bucked in his hand. Orange flame spewed from the barrel. A cloud of white smoke obscured his vision. The explosion boomed in his ears. He heard the low whine-spang of the lead ball as it slid across metal at better than a thousand feet per second.

The short assassin was gone when the smoke cleared.

Raider kept running, the ache in his side diminishing as he caught his second wind. His blood raced, and the searing pain in his lungs subsided. He had his man now, he thought. Close.

He rounded the ore car and slowed, cautious in the darkness.

He listened for a sound.

A boot scraped across stone and grit.

He heard the heave of something striking the ground.

Then a metallic click. Like a shotgun being broken open. A split second later there was the clatter of empty shells striking hard ground. More clicks; Raider strained to locate the direction from which they came. He had no doubt that the small man had reloaded his shotgun.

Death waited somewhere in the shadows of the yard. Raider could taste it in his mouth, smell it when he breathed through his nose.

A foot crunched on loose gravel.

Raider hugged the cold skin of the ore car, presenting no silhouette, making no sound.

He stooped down carefully, slowly. His fingers sought a chunk of stone, anything big enough to make a noise. His hand brushed against a rusted railroad spike. He stood up, gripping it loosely in his fingers.

His arm moved, sweeping upward in an arc. He lobbed the spike out into the open beyond the ore car, near a silent freight car.

The spike hit the ground with a thud, jarred pebbles loose.

The shotgun roared.

Lead peppered the sides of the freight car, rattled gravel, peppered the rail underneath. An orange light flashed nearby.

Raider stepped out into the open and crouched, his hammer thumbed back.

He fired just underneath the smoke. Once, twice, the pistol alive in his hand.

Then he dove for the ground. As he hit, he rolled toward the protection of the freight car.

The second blast swept the ground where he had stood. He felt the heat from the blast. The wad slapped against his arm where it met the shoulder, stinging the skin.

Raider looked up.

The short man was silhouetted atop a car, his shotgun empty.

Raider scrambled to his feet as the shotgun cracked open.

He started running at top speed for the car, the ladder on the side.

Seconds sped away as he raced for the ladder.

He never made it.

Just before he reached out to grab the rail, a figure stepped out from between two cars, blocking his path.

Raider saw him clearly. Part of him. His bald head glistening in the dim light from the yards.

He didn't see what was swung at him.

Instead he heard a crack like a melon breaking open. Lights danced in his skull. Pain shot through him like a prairie fire in a high wind.

And then he fell through inky blackness, past the pain, past all feeling, even as the ground rose up to meet him, slamming him full force into oblivion.

Doc looked into Janet's blue eyes and smiled.

"So you see, my dear, you can be of more help to us if you stay on at the mint."

He swept up the last of the roast beef gravy with a wedge of biscuit, swabbing his plate clean.

"But what about my father?"

"I'll take care of that. Don't worry about a thing."

"Why, I . . . I don't know what to say, Dr. Weatherbee. You're so kind. And you know so much about me and my situation."

"It's my business," he said, gloating with satisfaction.

"How can I ever repay you?" she asked innocently.

"By having a nightcap with me."

"You mean . . . ?"

"In my room."

"Why, Dr. Weatherbee," she cooed. "I don't know if that would be quite proper."

"I'll get you back to your boardinghouse in plenty of time," he said, his penetrating eyes fixed on hers. "I think you might be pleasantly entertained."

"If . . . if you think it's all right."

"Perfectly, all right, Janet. Trust me."

The quaint French restaurant on 17th had the electric lights turned down low and candles on the tables. Doc saw to it that their bill did not exceed his ability to pay with his dwindling funds. Even though the meal was chargeable to his expense account, it might be months before he was reimbursed. The Pinkerton brothers were every bit as stingy with money as had been their illustrious father.

La Petite Maison had been the perfect place to impress and seduce Janet Logan. Doc had explained the situation to her, without revealing any company secrets, and she had seemed duly impressed. Doc had laid his plans well. Janet Logan was as ripe as a peach and was being wasted on young, inexperienced swains who were still rather sodden behind the ears.

Doc had the maître d' wrap a bottle of inexpensive Bordeaux and put it on the bill. Bill Pinkerton would have a fit, but Janet would have her nightcap. Doc felt all was right with the world. Abernathy was on a train to Washington, and Raider was giving Welch a going-over. The night belonged to him. He had earned it. Despite the death of a good operative, Lucas Skye, he felt they were making progress in their investigation.

The Capitol Hotel near Colfax and Broadway was decent and not too expensive. Doc would have preferred to have stayed at the Windsor, in one of its three hundred rooms, but it was beyond his financial reach at the moment. He had walked through it, of course, and marveled at the three elevators and a ballroom floor suspended by cables to give it bounce when the orchestra played and the dancers cavorted. He had peeked into the baths, called a "sudsatorium" by H.A.W. Tabor and his cronies. There was also a "frigidorium," and a "lavoratorium." The menu in the main dining room featured frog's legs, guava jelly, prairie chicken, trout, venison, and bear meat, as well as real ice cream from the Windsor's steam-powered freezer. Although Denver now boasted electricity, the rooms in the Windsor were all illuminated by gaslight.

The Capitol was less elegant, but every bit as discreet.

The room clerk did not seem to notice Janet Logan, who hung back demurely as Doc picked up the key to his room.

Weatherbee's room was at the end of the darkened hall. He held Janet's hand as he led her to his door.

She did not seem reluctant to accompany him.

Gaslights made the room flicker with shadows, flashed on the flocked red velvet walls, glimmered on the desk, the table, the three chairs. Doc turned the flame low, brought two glasses to the table, and unwrapped the wine. He doffed his derby and hung it on a clothes tree of wood and brass. He loosened his gold silk vest and poured the glasses three-quarters full.

"Make yourself comfortable," he said, pulling out a chair for her.

Janet wore a plain blue frock with bows at the sleeves and collar, black stockings and short-heeled shoes, and a small cloche hat. She took off her hat and set it on the table.

Doc moved his chair next to hers and sat down.

He lifted his glass.

"Here's to you, Janet," he said. "And a long career at the mint."

"I don't want to work at the mint," she said. "I just don't want to live with my father."

"Too strict?"

"Yes. He . . . he's mean."

"Mean?"

"Pinch-minded."

"Ah, I see. You want to be a wild creature, and Papa puts too much harness on you."

"You have a funny way with words."

"Drink, my dear, and I'll listen to you."

Janet clutched her glass and brought it to her lips. She was already giddy from the wine at the meal. Her eyes danced with light, glittered at the closeness of Doc, who leaned toward her, stretched his arm to touch her glass with his.

The glasses clinked together.

They drank, looking into each other's eyes.

"You want me to talk?" she asked, slightly tipsy.

"Yes. Talk and talk, while I gaze at your loveliness. While I drink in your rare beauty."

"You talk pretty."

Doc's hand drifted under the table.

His hand found her knee and began to inch up her dress until it was exposed. He fondled her knee and looked into her eyes as Janet spoke about her life, her hopes, her dreams. Her voice kept getting softer and softer, while Doc's hand went higher up her leg.

Janet squirmed as Doc's hand wedged between her legs, pried them apart. He moved still closer.

"What are you doing to me?" she asked.

"Finding you," he smiled.

"You're very naughty."

"Yes."

His hand slipped inside her panties, touched the furred lips of her sex. She was wet. His finger parted the lips, stroked the velvety inner lining of her pussy. Janet squirmed again. Her mouth opened. Her tongue slid over his lips, smearing them with moisture.

Doc's finger jabbed gently into her love tunnel, triggered the tiny hardening clitoris.

Janet shuddered with a sudden spasm.

When she was primed, he took her in his arms, then began to undress her. She submitted willingly, panting with desire. Her legs quivered as he stripped down her panties, added them to the puddle of clothes on the floor. She began to undress him frantically, her fingers flying at the buttons, her hands tugging at his vest, his shirt, his trousers.

He laid her on the bed and gazed down at her naked body.

Her eyes glazed over as he entered her, plunging deep

inside her cunt on the first sure stroke.

She arched her back and thrust her hips upward.

He sank into heat, wetness; felt the squeeze of her muscles. His swollen cock throbbed like a sausage about to burst.

She cried out as the first spasm rippled through her loins. Doc skewered her on his rock-hard cock and she screamed as the climax built, shuddering through her with a volcanic ripple.

"Yes, yes," she moaned. "It's so good."

Doc did not relent but stroked her fast and deep, plumbing the depths of her pussy with his swollen probe. She bucked in orgasmic spasms, raked his back with desperate fingers. She threw her legs high in the air and drew him deeper until his cock penetrated the very mouth of her womb.

His mouth found a breast, gobbled the nipple, tongued it until it grew hard as an acorn. His hand massaged the other as he rose up and down over her pliant, squirming body, his cock shooting deep into moist hot folds of yielding flesh.

"More, more!" she exclaimed, as Doc backed off, staying his own climax.

She was a wanton, as he had known she would be, but her energy surprised him. She wrapped her legs around his waist, rocked with him in coital rhythms that jingled the bedsprings, rattled the brass posts.

Their bodies glistened with sweat, bronzed by the glow of gaslight.

"What a man," she breathed. "You do things to me no one else has done."

He rammed hard then and felt her buck with the jolting orgasm.

Janet let out a shriek that rattled the walls of the room.

Doc felt himself being swept up in her passionate ecstasy. He felt a rush of pleasure tingle through his veins. At the height of his own climax the door to the room boomed with the insistent pounding of a mighty fist.

It was too late to stop.

Doc spewed his seed as the knocking grew louder, his loins quivering with release.

Janet squeezed him in her arms, met him on the pinnacle, oblivious to the increasing noise at the door.

Doc cursed under his breath.

"Who is it?" he gasped, shuddering a last time as his sperm drained from his cock.

"Raider, you bastard! Open this fucking door or I'll break it down!"

Janet's eyes widened in startled surprise.

"My god," she breathed.

"No, we aren't that lucky or as close to the end of our days. It's only Raider."

He slid from her sweat-soaked body.

"In the wrong place at the wrong time, as usual," he muttered.

CHAPTER SEVEN

Raider massaged the lump on his forehead. It didn't help. His head throbbed like a roomful of bass drummers. The bouncing wagon didn't do him any good either, but Doc had insisted on bringing the Studebaker and Judith to Welch's Undertaking Parlor on Gilpin. Now, after wrestling with the traces for half an hour, they were on their way. He felt like wringing Doc's neck. While he was out getting shot at and getting his brains knocked out, Doc had been putting the boots to that Logan girl, who was half his age at least.

"You got a good look at the short one?" Doc asked.

"No. I got a good look at Baldy."

"So there are at least three of them in Denver."

"I figure, if what Luke said was so."

"Luke didn't make mistakes like that."

"He made one."

"Had to be the shorty who killed him too. Luke didn't see him until he was right on him. And we were probably looking too high."

"Yeah," said Raider, in no mood for any more questions. He had walked right into it at the railroad yards. The outfit was pretty slick. He had a pretty good idea why they had killed Abernathy. They wanted those personnel records. Whoever had pulled off the robbery of the silver was trying to cover up all tracks. Yet, they had left one—the Pecos dollar.

"Welch is just about our only hope right now. He knows who those robbers were," said Doc. "At least one of them."

"How you figure that?"

"He loaned his hearse out that night to haul off the hundred thousand."

"So?"

"So at least one of the bandits had to contact him. Before or after."

"Okay. If you say so, Doc. But why are we wasting time with this wagon? You going to sell medicine to Welch?"

"I'm going to call Wagner, and I don't want to go through the telegraph office."

Raider rubbed his forehead again. What he needed was a cold compress, a bottle of whiskey, and a good night's sleep.

"How was she, Doc?"

"Who?"

"Logan."

"Fair, Raider, just fair."

"Bastard."

The undertaking parlor was dark, but they could see the sign over the stone front. Since Denver had been almost burned down two decades before, flammable wooden buildings had been forbidden. Doc pulled Judith to a halt and set the brake. The two men climbed down and circled the building.

The loading dock was lighted out back. Three hearses sat silently in the barn. Horses nickered as they passed the stables. Electric lights burned inside.

The double doors were locked.

Raider pounded on them until someone opened them.

"Do you have a need?" asked a wizened watchman.

"We want to see Welch," said Doc.

"He's quite busy."

Raider swept by the man. Doc followed.

"Where is he?"

"Sirs, Mr. Welch is engaged."

Raider sniffed the air and smelled the sickly sweet aroma of formaldehyde. He saw a pair of doors, their windows lighted, and he made for them. Doc took only a moment to quiet the watchman's querulous pleas for dignity, then followed in Raider's wake.

Raider felt his knees go weak when he entered the preparation room. A woman in a pale smock, with a billowy cap on her head, looked up at him from the cosmetologist's table. She wore a surgeon's mask over her face, and he could see only her startled eyes.

Abernathy had been stripped naked and lay on a tilted slab table. He had been eviscerated and sewed up with leather. The stitches made a large Y from his shoulders to a spot midway down to a point just below the rib cage. The straight line from there ended at the base of his abdomen. The shot holes peppered his mortified flesh, and the belly stitches were ragged where the blast had torn him apart.

Bile rose up in Raider's throat when he saw the tubes inserted into the jugular vein of Abernathy's neck, and two more tubes attached to his ankle. Gutters under the table, on the floor, ran with blood as the mortician pumped the veins, filling them with embalming fluid. Abernathy's face was partially covered by a blood-soaked towel. The part that was visible had shot holes in the skin. A fragment of shattered tooth jutted out from under the towel.

"Welch?" Raider squeaked.

The mortician thumbed over his shoulder toward another set of doors.

"Feel pretty mortal, don't you?" cracked Weatherbee to Raider.

"Come on. Welch must be up front."

They entered a dark room full of caskets on stands. Beyond, an office light showed them another doorway.

Roger Welch sat at a desk filling out papers. Raider saw why the front was dark—the windows were covered with heavy drapes that were pulled tightly shut. Welch looked up when they came into the room, their footfalls silent on the heavy carpet.

"Are you from the mint?" he asked. A telephone—what Denverites called "galvanic muttering machines"—sat on the desk next to a quill pen in its holder. The rolltop desk was neat, the office itself quietly elegant, with its polished wood furniture, its expensive decor. "I only called a short while ago."

Welch was in his forties. He stared at them with close-set eyes framed by horn-rimmed spectacles. His sideburns were neatly trimmed, his hands smooth and delicate like a surgeon's. His skin had a waxy cast to it; it was flabby from self-indulgence. His cheeks were laced with spiders that indicated he loved his wine. He wore a discreet dark suit and a high-collar shirt with a silken bow tie dripping onto his chest. His cuffs were pinned with gold studs. He had all his hair, and it looked as though it had been dyed to erase the gray.

"You might say that," said Weatherbee. "We've come to talk to you about that hundred thousand in silver that was stolen off a freight wagon two years ago."

Welch blanched but kept his composure.

"I've already told the authorities that I know nothing about that robbery"

"One of your hearses was involved," said Raider.

"Stolen," said Welch glibly. "And while I regret Mr. Abernathy's passing, I am only the undertaker. I had nothing to do with his unfortunate demise."

Something was bothering Raider, but he couldn't put his finger on it. He let Doc handle the rest of the questioning while he tried to isolate a vagrant thought scratching at the edge of brain.

"Look, Welch, if you're afraid of somebody, tell me. We'll see to it that you're protected." Doc's voice dropped to a tone of confidentiality.

Welch wasn't buying it.

"I'm not afraid of anyone," he said stiffly. "You gentlemen are wasting your time."

"What's Baron von Richthofen to you?" asked Doc. A shot in the dark.

Welch looked discomfited. His lips tightened together and his eyes flickered. He shifted his gaze slightly so that he was no longer looking Weatherbee straight in the eye.

"I don't believe I have to answer your questions. Who are you anyway?"

"Never mind that. We have an interest."

"A strong interest," said Raider, suddenly shifting his attention back to Welch. The man was going to be a hard nut to crack. He moved closer, stood towering above the mortician.

"I've already told the authorities all I know."

"You're beginning to sound like a parrot," said Doc. "Who told you to pick up Abernathy?"

"Someone called from the station."

"You bring the body in?"

"No. Abernathy is well known. We are the undertakers of choice."

"Oh, then he made prior arrangements?"

"Yes, you might say that. He was a widower. We handled the arrangements for his wife."

"He have any other relatives?"

"I don't know. I don't think so."

Weatherbee knew that Welch was lying, but he didn't know why. He looked at Raider, temporarily halted in his interrogation.

Raider felt that odd scratching at his mind again, as if something important was trying to climb up out of a hole and gain his recognition.

"You bury any of the men killed that night of the robbery?" asked Raider.

"We took care of Leonard Brown."

"Know him?"

"No, his widow made the arrangements."

"You know her?"

"Only in a business sense."

"Don't smirk," said Doc, jumping in again. "You're not out of this yet. I think you know a hell of a lot more than you've told anyone about that robbery. What about Naylor?"

Welch's eyes flickered. Again his lips tightened to a thin slit across his face.

"He . . . he worked here as a swamper for a time. A very short while."

"You know he found the bodies that night?"

"He says he did."

"You don't believe him?" Doc leaned over so that he was close to Welch's face. Raider moved away and began walking around the office. There was a bookcase with a lot of technical manuals, *Gray's Anatomy, Embalming: The Art of the Egyptians,* and the like. A diploma from a medical school back east, an aquarium with goldfish and guppies in it, a brace of flintlock dueling pistols, and shelves with pickled organs. He gathered this was not the office Welch used to greet bereaved relatives of his clients. This was where he did his work, and Raider was curious as to why he felt it necessary to work this late. Another mortician was taking care of Abernathy's corpse, and the cosmetologist seemed ready to make the dead man look halfway decent.

"Naylor, ah, has a vivid imagination," said Welch. "He tends to exaggerate and, when in his cups, which is frequently, he is an outright prevaricator."

"Did you know Naylor was dead?" asked Raider, completing his circular tour of the room. He spun a global map of the world on a stand next to Welch's desk.

"Why no, but I'm not surprised. He had an enlarged liver and it was hard as a rock."

"But he left here and went to work for the baron," persisted Weatherbee. "Did you recommend him?"

"Certainly not!"

"It happened shortly after he said he saw the same hearse used in the robbery at von Richtofen's estate."

"Coincidence," said Welch quickly. Too quickly.

Raider was running out of patience. He wanted to jerk Welch out of the chair and shake the truth out of him. He gave the globe a swat with the heel of his hand and set it spinning rapidly. He stepped toward the moritician, anger boiling up in him.

The telephone jangled, the clapper striking the bell with

an insistent surge of electricity. Welch twitched, startled by the unexpected sound. Quickly he reached for the instrument. Raider stopped in his tracks. Doc stood up straight.

"Welch here," the mortician said into the mouthpiece. A tinny voice rattled the membrane in the earpiece. Neither Doc nor Raider could make out any of the words.

Welch's face drained of color.

"I'll be right there," he said.

He hung up the phone and rose from his chair.

"If you'll excuse me, gentlemen, there's someone waiting to see me in the front parlor."

The Pinkerton men exchanged glances.

Welch left the room.

"What do you think, Doc?" asked Raider.

"He's not going to crack. Give him two minutes and we'll check up on him."

"Mighty good timing on that telephone call."

"Yes. Front parlor. So someone either knows we're here or he's got a client."

Raider's expression changed.

"They wouldn't call from inside the building," he said. "Come on, Doc, I don't like the looks of this. The only client Welch has is Abernathy, and he's not supposed to have any kin."

Doc needed no urging. The two men moved quickly into the hall, Raider in the lead. Doc followed after with matching strides. They passed a series of doors and came into a large outer office. Beyond was another hallway. A cone of light spilled through a door and glistened on a thick rug.

Raider stopped when he heard Welch cry out.

"No, don't!"

Then there was a sound.

A man groaned in pain.

Then another sound, like a fist thudding into wood.

"Ooohhh, no!"

Doc shoved Raider into action. The two men moved toward the light. Raider rushed through the doorway.

Welch staggered toward him, a dagger in his belly. His

shirtfront was soggy with a spreading crimson stain. Raider reached out for him as Doc came up behind him.

Part of the parlor was bathed in shadow. A single lamp burned over a small writing desk with a phone.

Something moved in the shadows.

Doc saw it first.

A tall woman wearing a veil swept past them. They couldn't see her face.

"Stop her!" yelled Raider as Welch pitched forward into his arms. Doc tried to get around the two men. Raider's knees bent under the unexpected weight.

The woman turned as Doc came at her.

Doc reached out for her as she stepped in close.

He wasn't prepared for what happened next.

She drove a fist straight into Doc's Adam's apple, then rammed a knee into his groin. He doubled over in pain. He tried to yell, but only a squeak came through his larynx. His testicles swelled in an agony of hurt. He doubled over, feeling as if his balls had been shoved up into his abdomen.

The woman wheeled and was gone.

Neither Pinkerton had seen her face.

"Who was that, Welch?" asked Raider, turning the man over in his arms.

Roger Welch looked at him with a fixed stare. His eyes did not move.

Doc staggered to a spindly-legged chair. His throat ached, and the pain in his genitals flowered through his loins like fire.

"I know one thing," he croaked.

"What's that, Doc?" asked Raider, letting Welch's body slide to the carpeted floor.

"She's a bitch. A pure bitch."

CHAPTER EIGHT

Doc stopped the Studebaker wagon fifty feet from the telegraph pole. The pain in his groin had subsided, but his throat felt as if someone had filed it raw. Raider had searched all around the funeral parlor but had found no trace of Welch's assassin. Neither the mortician nor the cosmetologist had heard anything. They had no idea who could have murdered their employer. Nor did either Doc or Raider have a clue. It was another mystery piled upon a gathering stack of mysteries. They agreed on one thing: The woman was taller than most, and she was a cold-blooded killer.

Five minutes ago they had passed a honey wagon, and the stench clung to the air like the cloying afterwash of a latrine. Doc had purposely gone to an ill-lighted section of Denver so that he could tap into the telegraph wires and send his message to Wagner. Raider was impatient, because Weatherbee had spent a good half hour transcribing notes of their interview with Welch and his subsequent death.

"Still smells to high heaven," said Raider, climbing down from the wagon.

"Body wastes are as natural as prairie grass," philosophized Doc.

"It's still shit."

Doc stood up and turned to go inside the wagon.

"Better check out that pole, Raider," he said, disappearing through the opened flap. The telegraph office had been closed, but Doc knew there was a man sitting by his key somewhere along the line.

Inside, Doc lighted a lantern and hung it on a hook. He

peeled back a section of rug on the floor to reveal a hidden hatch. He raised the hatch and lifted a Western Union solid steel lever and trunnion onto the main floor of the wagon. He groped for his telegraph key, found its wires, and pulled it into the light. The nickel-plated trunnion gleamed silvery under the lantern spill. Next, he hefted the six-by-eight gravity battery, which weighed about seven pounds and was constructed of zinc, copper, and blue vitriol.

Doc hooked up the wires to the key and snuffed out the lantern. He could hear Raider pacing back and forth outside. Raider hated to climb telegraph poles.

Doc lugged the paraphernalia to the front seat and stacked it all neatly to one side. He stepped through the flap and climbed down.

He saw Raider's silhouette. There was a piece of moon and stars shining in a clear cloudless sky. Somewhere down the lonely street a dog barked for several seconds. A light fluttered on, and then it was quiet.

"Shit, Doc, hurry it up," said Raider.

"Patience. You could grab the battery. Be careful."

Reluctantly, Raider came over to help Weatherbee carry the gear to a spot at the base of the telegraph pole.

"One of these days, Doc, I'm going to climb up there and get electrified and you'll have to come up and get me down."

"Electrocuted," corrected Weatherbee.

"That, too."

Raider found a pair of climbing spikes in the back of the medicine wagon and strapped them onto his boots while Doc hooked up the wires and checked his battery.

"Ready?" Raider asked.

"Shinny up there and let's go," said Doc.

"Yeah, just like that."

Raider looked up at the pole. Each one seemed higher. He felt like a damned monkey. He took a stance, lifted one spike, and dug it in. When he was well started he turned and took the wires and tools Doc held out to him. He secured them to his belt and began to climb. Once at the crosstree he began to work fast. He didn't look down. He set the clamps.

"Go," he told Doc. "And make it short."

Doc began tapping his key. The wires hummed with electricity.

Dah dit, dih dah dit, dih dih dah, dih dih dit ... clattered the key, clearing the line for a priority message.

Doc was fast. His thumb was a blur on the key.

WAGNER, CHICAGO, PINKERTON AGENCY. PRIORITY MESSAGE FOLLOWS. WEATHERBEE. Doc slipped on his earphones, heard the responding code. Wagner was there. He was always there. Night or day. Doc wondered if there really was such a person or if Wagner was just a code name for the whole bunch of them in the Chicago office. He tapped out his code.

ABERNATHY MURDERED. DITTO OPERATIVE SKYE. THREE SUSPECTS. IDENTITIES UNKNOWN. SHORT MAN, BALD MAN, TALL YOUNG WOMAN. UNDERTAKER KILLED BY WOMAN. KNIFE. BARON VON RICHTOFEN MAY BE INVOLVED. ASSAY SHOWS SAME SILVER CONTENT PECOS DOLLAR AS STOLEN SILVER. ADVISE. WEATHERBEE.

There was a wait of almost two minutes.

The high-pitched series of dots and dashes, Morse code, sang over the wires, rattling Doc's key and vibrating in his phones.

CHECK VON RICHTOFEN. ABERNATHY RECALLED D.C. THIS MORNING. NO WORD ON HIS MURDER. PROCEED. WAGNER.

Weatherbee acknowledged the message.

RECONFIRM ABERNATHY. OFFICIAL? IF SO, WHY? WEATHERBEE.

CONFIRMED. WILL CHECK REASON. OFFICIAL. HIGHEST PRIORITY. MUST LOCATE SOURCE OF PECOS DOLLARS SOONEST. WAGNER.

Doc wanted to say something to Wagner about his request, but he held his electric tongue. Instead he thought for a few moments. Raider had been so sure that Abernathy had been set up. But apparently the telegram was genuine. But something was wrong. Somebody didn't want Abernathy to get to Washington.

Raider looked down. Doc wasn't sending. Wagner wasn't either. The key was silent.

"What's going on, Doc?"

"Thinking."

"Think some other time. I don't trust these spikes much. I can feel the wood going soft on me."

"Hold your horses."

Raider said something that Doc couldn't hear. He had a pretty good idea what it was.

Doc worked the key again.

WAS ABERNATHY'S RECALL CONNECTED THIS CASE? WEATHERBEE.

There was a long pause before Wagner began sending again.

CHECKING. WAGNER.

Doc waited.

"Christ, Doc," said Raider.

"Patience."

"Patience, my ass. I don't like sitting up here with all these wires."

"Wagner's checking something."

"What's going on?"

"Let you know later. Here he is again."

The key rattled with Morse.

WASHINGTON MUM ON ABERNATHY. NO MENTION OF PECOS DOLLARS THOUGH. ASSUME NO CONNECTION THIS CASE. PROCEED WITH CAUTION. STAY AWAY FROM DENVER MINT. CHECK BACK HERE 24 HOURS. END. WAGNER.

Doc locked the key down and took off the phones.

"Bring her down, Raider," he called up.

Raider removed the conductor clamps, breaking the temporary circuit. He was down the pole a few seconds later.

"What the hell was that all about, Doc?"

Doc told him.

"There's a lot that ain't right," said Raider. "Something's bothering me about Abernathy, and I can't come up with it."

"You were so sure that telegram was a fake."

"All right, I was wrong there. But there's something else, something a whole lot bigger, and we're missing it."

"You're missing it," said Doc dryly, beginning to wrap the wires Raider had brought down. Raider stalked off, hobbling on first one foot and then the other as he removed the climbing spikes. He hurled them into the wagon as hard as he could.

Judith jumped.

Doc held his tongue.

Carriages stood along the boardwalk outside the Windsor Hotel. A small group of people had begun to form a queue as Doc and Raider strolled up. Doc was dressed in his Sunday best, his gray derby dusted and brushed, his vest shiny in silvery velvet, his boots shined. Raider was dressed neatly, and he was clean, if a little bleary-eyed. He had shaved for the occasion and had left his pistol with the desk clerk at the hotel.

Sun buttered the stone building, peached the windows, glazed the turrets a burnt orange. Shadows still lingered in the streets like the cast-off garments of night.

Horses champed at their bits and clawed the cobblestones in front of the east entrance. Drivers in livery garb sat stiff and proper atop the seats, top hats squared, jackets neat, boots gleaming black.

Doc approached the doorman handling the loading of passengers and presented him with embossed invitation cards in linen-weave envelopes.

"Yes, sir," said the tall doorman with military bearing. "Coaches are departing within the quarter hour for the Baron von Richthofen's estate at Montclair. Refreshments are in the lobby."

Doc took back the envelopes and slid them into an inside pocket of his coat.

"Thank you, Captain," he said. "We'd like to catch an early carriage."

"Very good, sir. If you will fall into the queue, I'll see to it that you board one of the first carriages to depart."

Doc and Raider took their places in line.

"You handled that slick," said Raider. "How'd you wangle those cards?"

"Quite easily. Telephone and bank. Denver is one of the most progressive cities in the nation. It wants to be noticed. It's stumbling all over itself. I chatted with a banker, spoke of large investment sums, mentioned that I wanted to acquire genteel property for my family. I described the baron's Montclair scheme to a tee, and invitations were forthcoming."

"You're sly. And, for a detective, *mucho* dishonest."

"Ah, Raider, you've at last put the proverbial finger on the essence of our dubious profession. You see, we operatives, detectives, agents, policemen, are all larcenous at heart. The thief and the detective are one and the same. We play a game of badges and bandits. The felon is on one side of the law; we are on the other, ostensibly. But in the final analysis, we are one and the same."

Doc had spoken low, so as not to be overheard, but Raider was not so discreet.

"Horseshit," he said loudly.

A woman with a parasol turned toward the Pinkertons, then quickly bowed her head under the concealment of her wide-brimmed sun hat.

Her companion frowned under walrus mustaches.

Doc glazed them both with a frosty look.

"Raider," he said. "Just think about it sometime. If we didn't work for the Pinkerton Agency we'd both be outlaws."

Raider looked down the street, and beyond, to the far mountains. He said nothing. The line started to move as the doorman directed people into waiting carriages.

Later, on their way to the baron's Montclair development, Raider, who had been staring out at the country east of Denver, looked at Weatherbee in the opposite seat and said quietly, "Doc, you know, sometimes you're too smart for your britches."

Weatherbee smiled, drew a fresh cheroot from his lapel pocket, and stroked it inside his lips, wetting the tip down well. He bit off the end and spat it through the window.

"Anyone mind if I smoke?" he asked.

"I do," said Raider with a ferocious leer.

The other passengers sat stiffly in their seats, suffering in the relative silence of the carriage rumbling over a prairie road.

The caravan of carriages sped through the wide gates of the von Richthofen estate. Banners flapped on tall staffs, lending an aura of medieval pageantry to the countryside. The baron himself, mounted on a fine thoroughbred stallion, galloped alongside in full riding regalia. A pack of lusty wolfhounds followed after him, graceful as gazelles. The baron doffed his jaunty Tyrolean hat with a pheasant feather stuck in its band; he smiled a warm greeting to his visitors. Raider watched the man ride by, admiring his horse and hounds.

The baron was one of the more colorful and flamboyant members of Denver society, yet he had never seemed to be able to carry out any of his grandiose schemes. He had arrived in Denver late in the 1870s and immediately began to attract attention with his enthusiastic flair for promoting bizarre land schemes.

His first farfetched pipe dream was a remote section of land south of Denver that von Richthofen touted as being a paradise. He built an elegant beer garden and laid a special railroad spur to haul prospective buyers in via train. No one bought either the idea or the location. So now, after other land schemes and precious-metal promotions had failed to make the baron any richer, he had put all his energy into Montclair. The imposing castle had taken two years to build. People were already saying that his English wife hated the castle and the guided tours that invaded her privacy, and some were already predicting that she would draw the nobleman back to England within the year.

The castle was a splendid sight as Doc and Raider alighted. It rose in crenellated splendor off the prairie, its high battlements and turrets imposing against the spacious blue Colorado sky. It was ringed with a wall made of the same square-cut stones that were used in the castle. A water tank and windmill stood above a smaller dwelling next to the castle.

"Looks out of place, doesn't it?" said Raider.

"Extremely."

The baron greeted all the caravan's members—potential customers—and dismounted. A stable boy took the reins of his horse. Another man took in the wolfhounds before the ladies could express their concern.

Doc made a beeline for the baron before anyone else could get to him. Raider came along right on his heels.

"A word with you, Baron," said Doc. "Privately."

"Sir, I have guests, as you can see. Do you have an invitation."

"We do," said Doc. "But we're with the Pinkerton Agency. I don't think you'd like the other guests to hear what I have to say."

"Quite," said the baron, his British inflection tinged with the heavy accents of his Prussian heritage. "Won't you come inside? We can discuss what you have to say in my study."

The baron was a burly man, with clear blue eyes, curly hair parted in two places, and bushy muttonchop sideburns that flared on either side of his chin. He walked with dignity, his shoulders straight, his polished riding boots carrying him forward with graceful strides. A boy opened the wrought-iron gate as guides led the prospective buyers on a tour of the estate. Raider heard one of the guides promise a woman that they would indeed go inside the castle.

The baron's study was elegant, the wood furniture gleaming with polish, the heads of exotic animals jutting from the walls over sporting arms, rifles, pistols, crossbows, spears, swords, and a longbow. There was a moose head, a Dall sheep, elk, deer, and buffalo.

"Have a seat, gentlemen, and state your business," said the baron in his thick gutteral accent.

"We'll stand," said Doc.

"Very well."

The baron sat down in a wing-backed chair and crossed his legs.

"I'll be brief." Doc moved in close so that he threw his shadow over the baron. Raider strolled about, looking over the books and trophies. He eyed the bar and its cut-crystal decanters filled with amber liquids and licked his lips. "Two years ago a hundred thousand silver dollars were stolen from the Denver mint. Recently your name has come up in connection with that robbery. Two men who may have been in on it were seen visiting you the other day by one of our operatives. That operative is now dead. So is a witness, a man named Naylor, who once worked for you."

"Yes. Quite a loathsome man, actually." The baron's expression did not change. His eyes seemed to be vacant of expression, the blue so pale they appeared almost colorless in shadow. "And I was approached by two men who made a proposal to me that smacked of illegality."

"Do you know their names?"

"Yes, I do. Albert Metz, an engraver, and a lackey named Grumbowski or something like that. A Pole."

"Grabowski?"

"I believe so, yes."

"What was their offer?"

"Trivial, really. They wanted me to invest in a silver mine."

"A silver mine? Here in Colorado?"

"Why no," said the baron. "It was in New Mexico. Really out of the question. However, it is well known that I am a strong backer of silver currency. I believe we have not achieved the boom."

"What did they offer as proof of the quality of their mine?"

The baron rose from his chair and went to a desk by the windows. He opened a drawer and pulled out a silver dollar.

He handed it to Doc. Raider came over and stared at it intently.

"A Pecos dollar," said Raider.

"Yes," said the baron. "That is the location of their silver mine. In Pecos Gulch, New Mexico. A new town, a boom town. But too far off the beaten path. There would have to be a hundred mines there for me to be interested."

"Did you know Metz or Grabowski at the time of the robbery?" asked Raider.

"I knew Metz, yes. It was he who left a hearse here that night. He said he had borrowed it from an undertaker who would be out to retrieve it."

"Why didn't you mention this before?" asked Raider belligerently.

"Because no one asked," said the baron without blinking an eye.

CHAPTER NINE

Doc knew he'd have to talk fast or Raider would be dead drunk before he had finished. His partner had that hard gleam in his eyes, and he had already cracked open the bottle of whiskey. The two men sat in Raider's room in the Curtis that Sunday evening, having walked there from the Windsor without saying a word to each other. The baron had not given them much else. He knew Abernathy. He had known Welch only slightly. Doc was satisfied that the baron had told them the truth about the hearse, the visit by Metz and Grabowski. And now they knew more than they had before. They knew where to find the others involved in the robbery. Pecos Gulch. Wherever that was.

"Raider," said Doc, lighting a cheroot he had been saving for just this moment. "We have a full day tomorrow. I've got to see Janet Logan's father and get him off her back. I want to talk to Willa Hastings, Abernathy's clerk, see what I can find out from her. She may recall which personnel records she pulled for Abernathy the day he was killed."

Raider took a swallow of whiskey. His eyes didn't water, nor did his face change expression. Doc cringed.

"Then where do you get this 'we' stuff, Doc? I don't have anybody to interview."

"I want you with me. We've got to check with Wagner and get down to Pecos Gulch. He'll want to know what we learned from the baron."

"What did we learn from the baron?"

"Plenty. Al Metz is the short man. The one who put two barrels of buckshot in Leonard Brown and probably the one who killed Luke Skye and that bum, Naylor. And he's definitely the one who killed Abernathy. You were an eye-witness to that."

Raider took another swallow and wiped his mouth. He glared at Doc with hard eyes.

"Not exactly," said the tall man.

"What do you mean?"

"I didn't actually see Abernathy killed. He went around the building with Shorty—Metz—and next I know he's on the ground."

"So? That's close enough."

"No, it isn't, Doc. That wasn't Abernathy that was killed."

Doc felt spiders crawl up the back of his neck.

"Say that again?"

"I said it wasn't Abernathy. It looked like him some, but it wasn't Abernathy. I got there before Metz was through with him. He came back and put another shot in the man's face. It just hit me this afternoon. I've been puzzling over it ever since we saw that stiff on the table at Welch's."

The spiders scurried off Doc's neck and his flesh turned cold.

"Maybe you'd better lay it out straight and steady," he said. "This is damned important, Raider."

"The man I saw down had a belly full of buck, but his face wasn't touched. We see them working on a man identified as Abernathy in that undertaking parlor. The dead man has a towel over his face. Over part of it. And I see holes in the part that wasn't covered up. Buckshot holes. Didn't clang any dinner bells at the time. It came back this afternoon."

"You're sure?"

"Dead sure, Doc. The man down was about Abernathy's height and build, and his features were close. But he was in pain and I didn't pay too much attention. But he was alive, and he didn't have a damned mark on his face. I don't think the dead hombre on that slab had any face."

Doc puffed his cheroot thoughtfully. Raider continued to drink, but he wasn't getting drunk. He, too, was thinking hard.

* * *

Willa Hastings, a tall, austere woman, fixed a baleful eye on Doc's derby. He had not removed it.

She wore her hair tied back in a severe bun. Strands of it tickled her jaw and her neck, but she ignored the minor irritant to focus on the larger one before her.

"I'd appreciate an answer to my question, ma'am. About those personnel records."

"I'm considering whether I ought to cooperate, Mr. Weatherbee."

"Dr. Weatherbee."

"Oh? What is your degree?"

"Mister's all right. Now, about those records. I need to know the names."

Willa, a spinster in her early forties, doodled on a sheet of foolscap with a graphite pencil. She looked out her door, which was situated so she could keep an eye on the other clerks, on whoever passed by on the way to Abernathy's office.

"I was very fond of Mr. Abernathy," she said tightly. "He was strict and kind and efficient."

"To you."

"What?"

"That's your opinion."

"That's my experience, Mr. Weatherbee."

"I'm sure he would approve," said Doc dryly.

"I don't know. You say you are one of those Pinkertons, but you told Mr. Abernathy you worked for the government."

"It was necessary."

"It was a lie, sir."

"A small one. A temporary one. All for the good of the U.S. Mint, Miss Hastings."

Willa Hastings sniffed the air in the room and turned away from Weatherbee toward the window. She was as slim as a barrel stave, but oddly graceful, like a giraffe feeding on the leaves of tall trees. Doc admired her loyalty, her toughness. He knew that such people seldom get the recognition they deserved. Willa had been with the mint a long while and had worked her way up into a position of responsibility. She was not married because she devoted her life to her job. Abernathy had recognized her qualities and promoted her to her present desk. Abernathy, he now realized, was quite a man. Probably not dead. Probably in on the robbery from the beginning. May even have masterminded it. But why? In the long run, a hundred thousand dollars was not very much. If it was split five or six ways, it was no money at all, considering risks. There had to be another reason.

"Was Abernathy a happy man, Miss Hastings?"

She turned to look at him. Her piercing glance was like the fixed stare of a hunting hawk.

"I assure you, I do not know the answer to your question. Mr. Abernathy did not çonfide in me concerning his personal life."

"You saw him every working day. Worked closely with him. Did he ever seem, ah, preoccupied? Especially after the robbery. Did he seem upset that so much silver had been stolen?"

The question was finally the right one. Willa looked beyond Doc to a fixed point on the wall.

"Yes, he was upset. He felt very badly about those poor men who had been killed. He was terribly concerned about the loss of all that money. It was a blot on his fine record. He was very conscientious. Very. He...he was greatly disturbed over the whole incident. So were we all."

"And so he got the telegraph message and had you pull some personnel records. Was one of them Grabowski? And the other, perhaps, Metz?"

"Yes, those were two of them. And one other."

Doc fought to keep his eyebrows from rising.

"Three records?"

"Correct," she snapped.

"And who, might I ask, was the third one?

"Lorelei Standish."

"Who is Lorelei Standish?"

Willa Hastings looked away from the wall, straight at Doc. Her eyes went wide, went blank.

"You know, that's odd. I have no idea. I'm familiar with most everyone who's worked here at the mint. But—and I thought it curious at the time—I do not recall her. Not at all."

"Did you happen to glance at her record when you took it out of the file?"

Miss Hastings dropped her head. Her cheeks rosed over with the flush of embarrassment.

"I regret to say I did."

"And?"

"I only glanced briefly at her file. Mr. Abernathy was in a hurry, poor man."

"What did you see?" Doc moved in close, his eyes glittering now with interest.

"She . . . she worked here only a month. Before the robbery. Temporary. She was released the day before the . . . the robbery."

"Released?"

"Fired, sir."

Doc sucked in a breath. He was getting somewhere. But he didn't know where.

"What was her job?"

"I wondered about that. I never saw her. Not once. Her job was listed as 'Assistant to the Director of the Mint.' I was shocked."

"Pretty big job. Is there such a title?"

"Yes. There are three men who hold it. Never a woman. Never."

"Would such a person have access to everything here? Be able to walk through the mint without question?"

"Of course."

"Where were you when this Lorelei was hired? Were you at work?"

Miss Hastings now looked up at the ceiling. Her expression changed. Her eyes sharpened their glint, and her facial muscles hardened.

"No . . . no, I wasn't. I . . . I was, now that you mention it, on a month's leave."

Doc started for the door. He had learned much more than he had expected. He had another name.

"And you came back to work, when?" he asked.

Willa Hastings gasped, clutched a spot midway between her breasts with a doubled-up fist, as if she needed to pound a stopped heart back to beating.

"The day . . . the day after the robbery," she rasped.

Doc tipped his hat to Miss Hastings. She deserved it.

"Thank you, Miss Hastings," he said. "You've been most helpful. I'll see to it that your cooperation is duly noted in my journal."

He walked past the desks, looking for Janet Logan. Her desk was empty. There was no sign of any activity there. It was clean, neat. He walked back to Hastings' office.

He leaned around the door.

"One more thing," he said. "Janet Logan. She's not at her desk. Is she ill?"

Willa stood at the window, staring out at the Denver skyline. She turned, and her face was pale, as though dusted with a fine patina of flour.

"Miss Logan? Her father met her when she reported to work this morning. She tendered her resignation on the spot."

"I'll be double damned," muttered Weatherbee.

"I beg your pardon?"

"Nothing. I'll be going." Doc's stomach churned. He felt badly about Janet Logan. Well, that was life. He couldn't control much of it. He wondered if Janet would think he had betrayed her. Branfield Logan was the real villain. He had broken a promise.

But Janet would not think so. She would blame him.

There was no time now for regret. He had much to convey to Wagner—and then there was Pecos Gulch. Somewhere in New Mexico. Somewhere near Santa Fe.

Somewhere near hell.

* * *

Raider half dozed in the barber's chair. He lay there, his face swathed in a steaming towel, flat on his back listening to the buzz of conversation. Strong hands rubbed the towel against his skin, softening up his face. He heard the barber swirl the brush against the lathering soap in its mug.

An hour before, he had soaked in a hot tub, his head throbbing with the dull pulsations of a man-sized hangover. Now the fur was gone from his tongue and his head was clear of fuzz. Four cups of strong black coffee had helped neutralize the booze still lingering in his system. He had drunk most of a quart of loudmouth the night before, until Doc had left in disgust to go back to his own hotel. He was supposed to meet him somewhere late that afternoon, but he couldn't remember where. It didn't matter. Doc would find him.

The chair tilted back to an upright position as the barber cranked the lever. Raider felt the towel unswirl, exposing his face. The heat had felt good, better than a woman's caress.

As the barber soaped up Raider's face with the brush, the Pinkerton man remembered where he was supposed to meet Doc. At the telegraph office.

The steel razor, sharpened to a fine edge, skimmed expertly over Raider's face, slicing the stubble off close to the skin. The sound was oddly metallic, as if his beard was made of wire. He blinked, adjusting to the sudden light after the darkness under the hot towel. He looked through the window of the shop, barely listening to the scratchy voice of the barber talking to the man in his chair about times gone by.

"Sixty-three was a dry year, dryer than a widow's cunt," droned the other barber. "Wind come up that spring and dried the ground even more. Them old pitch-pine roofs began to curl up. They had a fire department, all drawed up on paper, but wasn't really one."

"I heard about it," said the man in the chair, obviously not wanting to hear about it again.

The barber ignored him.

"Happened at three ayem, on April the nineteenth. A drunk kicked over the stove at the Cherokee Hotel. Wind blowing from all directions. Hell, everybody tried to keep that fire down, and then she just went. By dawn, there wasn't anything left of downtown. It was just a charred bunch of wood. I lost my shop, all my tools. Lost everything."

"Yeah, I heard it was bad."

Raider started to doze off again, when his barber lifted his chin and began scraping underneath. Raider's eyes focused on a man across the street, coming out of the Denver Dry Goods Company carrying a large bundle.

The man crossed the street, not at the corner, but in the center. His bald head was uncovered.

Raider's eyes narrowed.

He had seen that man before. The night he was chasing Metz.

He jumped out of the chair, flinging the sheet aside.

"Hey!" yelled the barber. "I almost cut your throat."

Raider took out a wad of bills and tossed them in the chair. He wiped lather from his face and ran toward the door.

"Come back! I'm not finished yet."

Grabowski looked up and saw the mustachioed Pinkerton running toward him. He wheeled and recrossed the street, running with long strides.

Raider stepped up his pace, but the big man was deceptively fast. Grabowski began to pull away. From behind him, he heard the snap of a buggy whip. He looked over his shoulder and saw a buggy pull away from a spot near the barber shop. He could not see who was driving. The horse headed straight for him. People in the street scattered like a flushed covey of quail.

"Shit," muttered Raider.

Grabowski lengthened his lead, knocking people aside in his flight. The buggy came on, wheels rattling over cobblestones. Raider heard the whip crack and he winced. The sound was like a shot from small-caliber rifle.

The big Pole ran into a man. He shoved him with his free arm. The man bounced off a post and reeled into Raider's path. The Pinkerton dodged him but lost more ground.

The buggy passed him, the horse straining at the traces, its nostrils flared to suck in wind.

Raider clawed for his pistol.

Someone in the buggy shoved the snout of a rifle though an opening in the black cloth top. The muzzle wavered, then drew a dead-aim bead on Raider.

The detective zigzagged and ducked. His pistol seemed to leap into his hand. He cocked it as it came clear of the holster. A wad of shaving lather dripped onto Raider's lips, giving him the appearance of madness, of slavering like a hydrophobic dog. People on the street stared at him. A woman screamed.

A shot rang out.

The rifle sprouted smoke and orange flame. A cloud of white smoke billowed into the air. The bullet fried a path next to Raider's ear. His stomach knotted up like a fist. His knees went weak

He bounced into a brick building, then quickly brought his pistol up to fire. A small child darted from nowhere, blocking his line of sight.

Someone yelled.

Grabowski turned and ran toward the slowing buggy. An arm reached out for him. The rifle barked again.

Chunks of brick stung Raider's face. Fine grit bit at his eyes.

Grabowski swung up onto the buggy.

Raider fired his pistol, bracing himself against the building. The bald-headed Pole twitched. His mouth flew open. He turned, his face contorted in pain, looking at Raider.

The bundle dropped from under his arm. Another pair of hands grabbed his shirt and pulled him aboard the buggy. The buggy picked up speed.

Raider took aim again.

The rifle spat fire and smoke, shot out soft lead that would smash a man's bones, rip through muscle and veins, blood vessels, arteries. Raider was already moving, diving toward the hard street. He felt something tug at this coat. He hit, rolled, came up with both hands gripping his pistol.

The buggy jerked and rolled up the street.

The bundle Grabowski had dropped tumbled toward Raider; it stopped in front of him with a rattling of paper.

Raider let his hands fall. He eased the hammer down with his thumb.

The buggy took the corner on one wheel. The sound of straining metal and wood grated on his ears, screeching along the feather edges of his nerves.

The buggy disappeared from sight.

Raider got up on one knee and savagely attacked the bundle.

New clothes tumbled out onto the blood-spattered cobblestones. Riding clothes. Trousers, shirts, a woman's skirt, all made of rugged material.

The Pinkerton shoved his pistol back in its holster and rubbed his swollen eyes.

He kicked at the pile of clothing.

People began to emerge from hiding places. They stared at him as if was a madman. He glared at them and they shrank away from him in fear.

"Sonsabitches," he cursed.

But he wasn't talking about the gapers.

The thieves had eluded him, and it would take him time to get on their trail, even if he hurried. One thing was sure. They weren't going to a party ball but into rough country. He had hit Grabowski, but even as he realized this was so, he knew the wound wasn't fatal. He had not heard the thunk of ball into hard flesh or bone.

A man knew when his shot was fatal.

A man like Raider knew. The way the Pole had twitched told him the man would live.

They would meet again.

CHAPTER TEN

Winton Spooner dipped his tea bag into the steaming water with delicate precision, as if he were weighing gold dust. He leaned over his cup and sniffed the aroma of the tea as it released its potency into the scalding liquid. He sat on the porch of the boardinghouse alone, his nearsighted eyes quivering behind corrective lenses set in gutta-percha frames. He wore khaki mufti and a pith helmet. His carpetbag lay like a swollen animal at his feet. A kit bag bulged with field glasses, picks, scales, a case of precision instruments, dog-eared manuals in dusty leather bindings, pencils, a pen, and a small wooden canteen that he could carry on his hip with the aid of bent metal hooks that fitted to his belt.

The afternoon sun lapped at his hobnailed boots and smeared the porch with a dirty yellow cast like vomit turned to dust. Flies buzzed and lighted on the sugar bowl set in the center of the table. Spooner shooed them away with flapping slender fingers as he dunked the tea bag in and out of his cup. Finally he let the bag, made of thin cheesecloth, sink to the bottom and steep.

Spooner was a geologist, more at home in rough, rugged country than in a ramshackle boardinghouse in Tucumcari, New Mexico. He was thirty-two years old, unmarried, and virtually homeless. His last job, for a lead-mining outfit, had been in Arkansas, where he had tramped through the Ozarks hills along the White River just below the Missouri border.

His hair was prematurely gray, and his features were boyish, with wide-set eyes, a thin straight nose, and a slightly receding chin.

The front door opened slightly. A woman stuck her head through the opening.

"Your party arrive yet?" she asked.

"No, Mrs. Hall."

"I thought I saw dust on the road."

Spooner looked down the road. She was right. There was dust. A long way off.

"Yes, I see it. Thanks."

The door slammed. Edith Hall was a snoopy women, and her meals were meager fare for a hungry man. Still, her boardinghouse was economical, and Spooner was no spendthrift, even on an expense account.

He shook sugar into his cup after removing the tea bag and stirred it with a spoon.

The wagon grew visible on the horizon, coming along slow but steady.

Spooner felt the tingle of anticipation. He sipped his tea patiently, mulling over the telegram that had reached him in El Paso two weeks before.

PROCEED TUCUMCARI STOP. MRS. HALL'S BOARDING-HOUSE. WAIT FOR WEATHERBEE STOP. ARRIVING AUG THREE (3) AFTERNOON STOP. RETAINER DRAFT FOLLOWS STOP. WILLIAM PINKERTON.

Of course Spooner knew who Pinkerton was. He had gone to school with Bill, had kept in touch over the years. What amazed him was that Bill knew where he was and that he was free after doing geological work in and around El Paso for the better part of a year. The retainer had been more than adequate. It had arrived by special messenger, and there had been specific instructions: One, he was to answer only to a man named Weatherbee, an undercover operative; and two, he was bound to secrecy. No one was to know where he was going, when he was leaving, or who had retained him. All mail would be forwarded to his ultimate destination, and all offers for his services would be handled through an agency familiar to William Pinkerton. At the close of his assignment he would be paid a lump sum equal to or better than his normal rates.

So Winton Spooner felt very smug that afternoon. He was employed, and someone was taking care of business for him in his absence. This was better than Boston by far. He had seen many interesting geological formations on the way to Tucumcari, and New Mexico was rich for such exploration.

The wagon drew up, and Spooner was shocked to see that it seemed to belong to an itinerant drummer of patent medicines. The legend on the canvas side proclaimed—

DOC WEATHERBEE'S PATENT MEDICINES.

Spooner's mouth dropped open.

And the man driving the moth-eaten mule didn't look at all like a man William Pinkerton would hire as a detective.

Doc grinned and pulled on Judith's reins. The mule stopped. Doc set the brake, knocked his pearl-gray derby back on his head, and drew a cheroot out of his vest pocket.

"You Spooner?"

"Why, uh, yes. I guess so."

"You don't know who you are?"

"I mean, yes, I am Winton Spooner."

"Weatherbee. Throw your gear in the back and climb aboard. We haven't got time to dawdle."

Winton Spooner just stared at Weatherbee.

"You're a Pinkerton?"

Doc's eyes rolled back in his head. "Well, I wouldn't want everyone in Tucumcari to know that just yet. Are you coming with me or not?"

Spooner thought about it. Doc lit his cheroot, seemingly in no hurry. He dusted his jacket off by patting it with hands worn smooth by the reins.

"I'll be right along," said the geologist. Mrs. Hall stuck her head out the door again.

"You leaving, Mr. Spooner?"

"Yes, I am."

"Goodbye. You come again."

"Thanks for the tea."

"Come on, Spooner," said Doc. "You can write her a letter. If you have time."

Spooner moved with alacrity, but not without a certain amount of awkwardness. He threw his carpetbag and satchel in the back and came around the front on the right side. The wagon started to move before he was quite aboard. Luckily the mule didn't move fast. He finally tumbled in, his legs dangling over the side. Doc reached down, grabbed him by the back of his collar, and jerked.

"I say," said Spooner. "What's the hurry all of a sudden?"

"Got to meet a man," said Doc. "If he's still alive."

"Who?"

"His name's Raider."

"Where is he?"

"A place called Pecos Gulch."

"I never heard of it."

"Neither did I," said Doc, dryly.

Raider had about six days of beard and at least two of hangover. He had run through two horses, one into Raton Pass, another before getting to Rancho de Taos; the third was the most jarring son of a bitch he had ever sat. He was sure the bastard had one leg made of wood, another made of stone. He had tried to get the animal into every gait he knew, from a single-foot to a lope, and the horse, a blue roan with one wild eye, seemed to get stuck in between, rattling his brains every time he put a hoof to ground.

Raider wanted to shoot him. Right behind the ears.

Or himself.

The man who had sold him had claimed he was a three-gaited pony. In a pig's ass he was. He had about ten gaits, and they were all bad. The California saddle, usually comfortable, had become an iron torture chair, crushing vertebrae, twisting hip bones, rattling something loose inside his skull. He had tried every position known to white man or Plains Indian, short of hanging upside down under the roan's belly, and not once had he found comfort.

Doc's mule, Judith, would have been a better ride, bareback, bony hump and all.

"You miserable son of a bitch," he railed. "Find a fucking

gait and stick to it. I ought to take a pole to your head and knock you senseless."

He shut up quick, as sparks flashed in his brain and whiskey pain juggled his head. Taos, a hell of a town, full of beautiful women and Indians and the worst whiskey he had ever tasted. Taos Lightning, they called it. Made out of wood sweat, tobacco, hot chili peppers, bad corn, old socks, and iron filings. It burned from throat to asshole and made a man think seriously about suicide. He had heard tales of it, and damn him, he'd just had to try it and see if he could beat it.

Stupid.

The best story he'd heard was of an old man putting a gun to a young man's head, handing him a jug of that Taos poison and saying, "Take a swig of this." The young man retched and vomited, choked and spluttered, but somehow got it down. Then the old man handed the kid the gun, grabbed the bottle from him, and said, "Now you hold the gun on me while I take a swaller."

Just the thought of Taos turned his stomach queasy. He wondered if he'd ever find a medicine to tame the curdling that kept reminding him of how mortal he was. None of Doc's nostrums or medicants had done the job.

Raider cocked his head and eyed the sun. Pecos Gulch could not be far now. And the town was *the* talk along the trail. Everywhere he'd been, men spoke of how wide open it was, how it reminded them of raw towns they had been in where every second man rode the owlhoot trail. Hard to imagine a town like that in this day and age, with the Hole in the Wall gang scattered and dead, the law's long arm stretching far and fast with rail travel as common now as horse apples in the road used to be.

But New Mexico was not civilization, although Taos bragged and Las Vegas whooped and Santa Fe boasted of their successful growth from a multitude of cultures. Underneath the skin of these towns there was still the pulsebeat of the untamed West. And Pecos Gulch, from the descriptions he had heard, was as wild as Abilene in the old days, as mean as Fort Worth or Dodge or Tombstone, with one extra ingredient—the killers there worked in the dark, without mercy. No shoot-outs at high noon in the middle of a dusty street—these were people who killed in cold blood, and a man's back was as good a target as his chest.

By late afternoon, Raider no longer had to speculate on what kind of a town Pecos Gulch was. It lay sprawled before him in the sun, nestled in a little valley that was broken up by low hills threading through it. Houses crouched on hillsides and teetered from rocks, cheap prefabs shipped in by wagon. There wasn't any wood. The Pecos flowed by, giving them water. The main street was lined with false fronts. He saw some tents on a slope. It was in a gulch, and at first glance appeared to be a mining town. At first glance.

Instead, as Raider rode along the gritty street, looking at signs, Pecos Gulch was a gambling, whoring, hell-raising town. Hardcases leaned against posts, watching him with ferret-quick eyes. Painted women waved to him from curtained windows overlooking balconies: Indians, Mexicans, Yankee women with hard pale faces that said they seldom saw the sun until late in the day when it had lost its force.

Raider's head had cleared. The queasy churn in his stomach had subsided. He had sweated out the poison. Most of it.

He would live.

Maybe.

He passed a half-dozen saloons, two gambling parlors, a butcher shop, a mercantile store, and a barber shop. Each establishment advertised "games of chance," no matter what its main line of business was. The only hotel in town that looked halfway decent was the Silver Dollar. There were bunkhouses aplenty, beds going for two bits a night and up.

Raider hitched up at the Silver Dollar's rail and stepped inside. Beyond the lobby he saw part of a long bar and heard the *swick* of cards and the clatter of poker chips. He heard a wheel of chance spinning on oiled bearings, low laughter, muffled voices, the clink of glasses.

The clerk didn't look at him close. He was an old man with poor eyesight, Raider decided.

"Room," he said.

"Ten bucks a night."

Raider whistled.

"Less'n you stay by the week."

"Then what?"

"Four bucks a night."

"Quite a drop. You got any two-dollar rooms?"

"What do you think this is, mister? Laredo?"

"In Laredo you could rent the hotel for two bucks."

"Suit yourself. Bunkhouses give you a bath, a cup of coffee, and a bed for that price."

"I'll stay a week."

"Put down whatever name you're using in that book there. Outhouse out back. We got a tub. Fifty cents for a bath. If you want a lady to scrub you down it's a extry two bucks and you can latch the door. You want a woman in your room, it's three dollars. The hotel keeps one."

"Is there anything you can't get in this town?"

"Yeah, there is, stranger. You can't get rich."

Raider put down a name. John Brown. There were four of them already, so he put a Jr. after his. The clerk didn't even look at the book. Raider gave him thirty bucks and got back two dollars and a room key.

"Top of the stairs, turn left, third door on your right. You got a good view."

"Of what?" asked Raider.

"Bawdy house out back. In the early part of the evening the gals take their cribs outside. Cooler there. You can watch; it don't cost you nothing."

Raider swallowed hard, thought about the binoculars in his saddlebags, then shook his head. He wasn't that far gone. He'd keep the shades down.

An hour later, after putting up the blue roan in the stables and paying for grain and hay with wincing reluctance, he had scraped hair off his face and bathed in cold water until his teeth had chattered. Hot water, he learned, was two bits extra. Wagner was going to scream about his expenses as it was.

Raider set his hat square and checked his image in the wavy tin mirror hanging on the wall. It was time to go to work.

A man named Jess Burnett noted Raider's entrance into the hotel and checked his room number. He was in the bar when Raider walked in an hour and a half later. It was Burnett's job to check on all strangers to the Gulch. As soon as Raider took a spot at the bar and ordered a drink, Burnett melted out of the room and went to the front desk.

"I'll have Brown's key," he told the clerk.

"Which one?"

Burnett looked.

"Junior," he said. He was a short, lean man with heavy eyebrows and almost no eyelashes. His pale blue eyes seemed to bulge out of their sockets as a result. He was wiry, quick, with delicate, uncalloused hands. He wore a pearl-handled revolver made by Sam Colt. It rode high on his belt, and he carried his hands belt-high all the time. He wore a dark shirt, canvas trousers, new boots, no spurs. The heels of the boots were built up to give him stature. He had bad teeth, and these were permanently dusky from the small wad of tobacco he kept in his cheek like a cud.

Burnett took the stairs two at a time, determined to rifle the stranger's saddlebags for a clue as to his identity, his origins.

Laura Lee Hope moved in as soon as she saw Burnett leave. She sidled up next to Raider at the bar and batted her eyes at him coyly.

Raider had just taken a sip of better-than-average whiskey. He looked down at the girl next to him and saw deep brown eyes, apple-plump cheeks, and a sad smile framed by a pair of dimples. She had hair the color of wheat straw, she didn't wear much rouge, and she had only a faint trace of vermillion on her lips.

"I came to drink," said Raider.

"Mind if I join you?"

"You paying for your own?"

"If you like." Her voice dropped low. He liked the husk in it. Or something in him did. Despite himself, he felt his loins warm with desire. The girl had a nice figure, not too much hip, enough buttocks to give a man a good handle when the going got boisterous. "I just thought you'd like to know that while we're talking here a man is up in your room, going through your luggage."

"I don't carry luggage." Raider chuckled. "Saddlebags."

"Your saddlebags, then. I hope you don't have anything in them you don't want Jess to see."

"Jess?"

"Jess Burnett. He's a kind of watchdog for Big Jake."

"That would be Loman."

"So you know him." She looked disappointed. Raider could have sworn she was pouting.

"No. Just heard about him. All bad."

"That's Big Jake. Look, I work for him. So does most of the town. I can't stand here talking to you unless I have a drink."

Raider had already decided what to do. First contacts could sometimes be important. This girl might be the enemy, but for the moment she was all he had. And he sensed an air of desperation about her.

"I'll buy you a drink," said Raider. "But I don't get the point. Unless you want me to walk up to my room and surprise this Burnett in the act of rifling my goods. In that case, either he gets out, gets killed, or..."

"Or what?"

"Or I get killed." Raider paused, watching her face carefully for a reaction. "Is that what you want? A little action? A little blood?"

"I don't understand," she said. But her breasts rose and fell with her deep breathing. The top halves of the mounds swelled, threatening to break out of their harness and flow over her bodice.

"Well, some women are like that. They like to start things and then sit on the side and watch two men club each other to death with fists, or shoot out each other's eyes."

Laura Lee shivered in the chill of his words, in the cold hard clutch of his eyes.

"I'm not like that," she said softly.

CHAPTER ELEVEN

Raider caught the bartender's attention with a beckoning flick of his fingers. The man came over.

"Bring the lady a drink," he said. "Whatever she wants."

"She's having—" the barkeep started to say.

"I said whatever she wants, man. Tea or whiskey, beer or sarsaparilla."

The bartender caught the tall man's meaning. He turned to the girl.

"What will you have, Laura Lee?"

She looked at Raider. A smile flickered on his lips.

"Whiskey," she said boldly, with a defiant toss of her head. "Real whiskey, for a change."

"You . . . sure?" The bartender looked at Raider and swallowed when he saw the glint in the Pinkerton's eyes. "Yeah, I reckon that'll be all right, Laura Lee. Whiskey."

The barman poured a straight shot in a small tumbler. He poured it from the same bottle Raider was drinking from and did it openly. But his eyes darted in their sockets as he gazed fearfully around the room. He walked away, leaving his mark on the bottle after Raider paid him in coin.

Raider turned to the girl.

"You got your whiskey, Laura Lee," he said quietly. "Now, just what is it you want?"

"You," she husked.

Her hand slid silent and unseen to his crotch.

Fingers caressed his bulge.

Raider felt his knees go weak and turn to gelatin. Her touch was soft, warm, gentle. Her eyes were wet, and her fingers trembled.

"You must be the highest-priced lady in Pecos Gulch to

touch a man like that," he said, moving away from her. "That shows training. Practice."

"Not for you," she said, her voice throaty with desire. "No charge. I think you might just be the man I'm looking for."

Raider sucked in a breath and held it. The woman was unnerving. She looked at him boldly now, and he could sense the hidden fire in her.

"To do what?" he asked.

"To get me out of the Gulch. I'm a prisoner here. Just as much as you are, stranger."

He swallowed hard and looked around the room. Men turned away from his gaze quickly and others dipped their eyes, avoiding his accusing, probing stare.

Raider felt something crawl up the back of his neck.

Laura Lee had put her finger on something, all right. He *was* a prisoner here. Of the Pinkerton Agency, of Big Jake Loman, of the town, and—of her.

Suddenly he realized why it had been so easy to ride in here, right smack in the middle of an outlaw town.

Admission was free. It cost nothing to get in.

It would cost dearly to get out—alive.

He swore.

"You have a place we can go? Can you get away?"

"I can go to your room. You lay a twenty next to that bottle and no one will say a word."

"You going to drink that whiskey?"

"No. I just wanted to see if you'd back me up. Charlie there's about to have a fit. Big Jake has a rule about his girls drinking."

"Not during working hours."

"Yes," she said, a weak smile playing at the corners of her mouth.

"And you're working."

"I just came on a few minutes ago."

"Twenty dollars is a lot of money for a little bit of pleasure."

"Not for information that might keep you alive."

"No," he admitted. He drank his whiskey. He looked at her glass. She nodded. He drank that too and felt it burn all the way down.

"Reckon Burnett's through up in my room?" he asked her.

"Yes. There he is, going back to report to Big Jake. I hope you didn't have anything up there that will get you in trouble."

"Like what?"

"Rumor has it that a couple of detectives are heading this way."

"Detectives?"

"Pinkertons. Big Jake wouldn't like that."

"No, he wouldn't, I guess."

She looked at him oddly. Raider fished out a twenty-dollar gold piece and flipped it on the bar. Charlie came over.

"How much for the rest of that bottle?"

"Five."

"Two."

"Three."

Raider gave him another three dollars and grabbed the bottle with one hand and Laura Lee with the other.

"Let's go spend twenty dollars," he said.

Burnett stopped before a door in the rear, looking at Raider and the girl. Raider turned at that moment and saw the man. There was disappointment on Burnett's face. Raider smiled.

There wasn't a thing in his saddlebags to connect him to the Pinkerton Agency.

Laura Lee started to strip out of her red satin dress after Raider lit the oil lamp on the sideboard.

"Not so quick," he said. "First, some information."

"Don't you want me?"

"We'll get to that when the time comes." Raider looked through his saddlebags. Burnett had been thorough, and he didn't leave much sign. He grabbed the bottle off the sideboard where he had set it when he lit the lamp; he looked again at the girl. "First, how did you get into this?"

"You mean why I came here?"

"That'll do for starters. Have a chair." Raider sat down and pulled the cork out of the bottle with his teeth. He drank straight from the bottle. He wasn't much on glasses in private. Laura Lee sat down and composed herself. Her skirt rustled like a thin sheet of tin.

"Big Jake. He... he made me come here."

"Made you?"

"I... I had run away from home, and he knew it. He... he said he was a minister."

"And you believed him?"

"He was a minister. I mean everyone said he was, and he had other homeless girls with him."

"Where was this?"

"Cheyenne."

Raider mulled that over. He knew that ought to mean something. But he hadn't given Cheyenne a thought. Denver, maybe. Or Santa Fe. What in hell was Loman doing in Cheyenne? And a preacher at that. He was probably missing something important. Maybe Doc would know something.

"So what happened?" he asked, the whiskey warm in his belly.

"I thought I was going to a house for homeless girls. In fact, it was. Then, one night, he said we had to leave. He had wagons, drovers. The next thing I knew we were in Santa Fe. We stayed there for a while. Big Jake—only we didn't call him that then—bought a lot of lumber and had it shipped out here. He told us he was going to build us a home and we'd love it. There were eight of us, but one girl ran away."

"Big Jake turn you out?"

"What do you mean?"

"He take your cherry?"

Laura Lee hung her head and blushed. She nodded, her lips trembling.

"You want him to?"

"I...I don't know. It...it happened so fast and all. I guess so, at first. I was flattered by his attentions. I didn't know he was doing it to the other girls."

"I can't wait to meet this bastard," said Raider under his breath.

"He...he was very charming at first, then when we came here we found out why he brought us along."

"Yeah. I imagine he wanted to build the town up pretty fast. You could get men to come here if you had some girls and the price wasn't too high."

Laura Lee wiped a strand of hair away from her face and took a deep breath.

"I'm not proud of myself. He said he'd beat us if we didn't do what he said."

"And did he?"

"Yes. Not me, though. But I saw Wanda's back where he had taken a quirt to her."

Raider winced. A quirt was a short whip with three strands of hard leather. It could lay open a man's back and raise some ugly welts.

"Who's Wanda?"

"The girl who ran away."

"What was Big Jake's name before?"

"Logan."

Raider's mouth twisted in a wry grin.

"Branfield Logan?"

"Why, yes. But he doesn't want to be called that anymore."

"Not much of a name change, from Logan to Loman. But might save him some trouble. Was he up in Denver recently? Within the last month?"

"Why, yes, he was gone. I don't know where."

It fit. Doc had told him about Janet Logan's father. The Reverend Branfield Logan. And she had gone with him. To Cheyenne, supposedly. Now he wondered if Janet wasn't the inside person who helped set up the silver robbery. They had completely overlooked her. Doc had to get in her britches and failed to check her out. Now there was going to be hell to pay.

"He bring anyone back with him?" Raider asked. "A girl? His daughter? Her name's Janet."

"Why, I don't know. I really don't. He doesn't exactly confide in me."

"So you ran away from home. Why?"

"I was in love with a boy. My father refused to let me see him. I hated him, and my mother too."

"What happened to the boy?"

"He . . . he didn't want anything to do with me after I left home. He wouldn't marry me. Said he wasn't ready to settle down."

Raider took another swallow of whiskey. Not too much. Just enough to clean out the cobwebs in his brain and wash the last of the trail dust away.

"And now you want to get out of here. The Gulch."

"Yes. Can you help me?"

"I don't know. I can try. If you're serious. If you're on the square."

"I am. Believe me I am."

There was more he wanted to ask her, but her lips were wet, and when she leaned over the table her breasts all but fell out of her bodice. Laura Lee was pretty, damned pretty, and he liked her perfume. He wanted her. But there was one thing he had to know first.

"What about the life you're leading. You don't like that?"

"Oh, yes," she said. "I like men. It's just that Big Jake doesn't pay very much. Another girl, who came here from Taos, said I could make a lot more money in San Francisco or Los Angeles."

"Christ! You mean that's why you want to get out of here?"

"Yes. I want to earn enough to go back home and see if that boy is ready to marry me."

Raider shook his head. He had heard the story before. A thousand times along a thousand trails. A girl thought she could earn easy money, save it, and then go back home and be respectable. She would tell everyone she had been a clerk or a secretary, and they would know, just by looking at her, what she had been. Well, some had done that, all right. Some had pulled it off. They said a whore made the best wife after she quit selling it and got married. A whore knew how to please a man. But Laura Lee wouldn't make it. The boy she had left behind no longer existed. He was probably no longer a boy. He might even be married. If Laura Lee kept working she would start to get hard inside, and what she did for a living would show on her face.

There were other Big Jake Lomans in Los Angeles and San Francisco. Pimps who would beat her and keep her broke so she'd have to keep working.

"What's the matter?" she asked when he hadn't said anything for a long time.

"Nothing," he gruffed. "Just get your clothes off. I want to see what I got for my twenty bucks."

Raider could see why Laura Lee was so anxious to peel out of her clothes. She had a body to be proud of, and there wasn't a mark or a blemish on it. She knew how to undress, too, taking her time, making each item of clothing seem like an important sacrifice. Whoever had taught her the trade had taught her well. By the time she was down to her black satin panties with the lacy edges, he had a throbbing hard-on and fire in his loins.

Laura Lee turned slowly, gracefully, to give him a long, lingering look at her body. Her skin was smooth, taut over fine bones. Her breasts jutted out from her chest like ripe melons, the nipples perky in the center of their dark areolae. Between her legs were a thatch of fine golden hair and a mound that seemed to bulge with swollen desire.

"I'll undress you," she said, and her voice had the purr of a hunting cat. "It's more pleasurable that way."

"Christ, yes," said Raider, mesmerizied by her body, by the high, proud lilt to her buttocks, the straightness of her legs, the thoroughbred trimness of her ankles. The woman seemed built to give a man pleasure, with just the right amount of flesh in the right places. The hemispheres of her butt were symmetrical, firmly plump. When she walked around in a little circle, as if she was modeling invisible clothing, he saw her ass move without wrinkling.

She touched him all over as she unbuckled his gunbelt and unbuttoned his trousers. Her fingers lingered intimately on his hips, between his legs, around his waist. When she took his shirt off, she pressed her warm body against his and rubbed her pussy against the bare bone of his knee. It was plain that Laura Lee not only loved her work but was accomplished at it. She led him to the bed, took off his boots, pulled his trousers the rest of the way off, and then slithered up his lean frame and kissed his neck, his ears, nuzzled through his mustache with her nose.

He grabbed for her, but she pulled away.

"No," she whispered softly. "You must let me excite you until you can't stand it anymore. Just sit still, and I promise you won't be disappointed."

"I can't stand it anymore already," he husked.

She laughed a dry, throaty laugh and slid down his body until she was squatted between his legs. She took his cock in her hands, and her touch was so delicate he could feel his cock swell against the palms—the hot palms that now began to move in small circles on either side of his shaft. She rubbed him that way as if she were kneading dough, as if she were gently massaging a sore muscle. Raider felt fresh blood rush through the veins of his prick, swelling it to the bursting point.

When he thought he could stand it no longer, she stopped her rubbing and he grabbed for her.

She pushed his arms away and bent her head. She buried her face in his groin, found his cock with her mouth. She shifted her legs so that she knelt before him.

Her tongue lapped at the crown of his prick, laving it with saliva. Raider stretched, pushed to bury it in her mouth. But Laura Lee took her own sweet time. She licked up and down the length of his shaft and all around it. She teased the tiny slit-hole in the head with her tongue, and Raider felt as if he were being turned inside out.

When he thought he could stand it no longer, she put her lips over the mushroom-shaped head and slid downward, burying his cock in her steaming mouth. She began to suckle him, her cheeks caving in. And her tongue kept flicking, licking, stroking the crown of his cock with a relentless expertise.

Her hand played with his scrotum, hefting the bag, gently massaging each testicle. Her fingers probed the base of his cock, applying pressure to a vein, then releasing it to let in fresh blood.

Raider watched her, felt her tits rub against his legs. Her hands were everywhere, her fingers touching his flesh like small hungry creatures without eyes or mouths. His scalp prickled and his loins raged with a savage fire. He reached down with one hand and stroked her hair. This time Laura Lee did not resist. She bathed his cock in warm saliva, and he began to pump into her, moving his hips in spontaneous coital rhythms as ancient as life itself.

She sucked him in deep, into her throat, and he felt the tip of his cock touch the opening. She held him there for only a second, then drew him back out.

She looked up at him with glazed eyes.

"Now you are ready," she said.

He dug his fingers into her hair, into her scalp, drawing her toward him.

She rose up from her kneeling position.

"Yes, godamnit," he croaked.

He hauled her onto the bed with strong, sinewy arms. She was pliant in his arms as he tumbled her over on her back. He spread her legs, mounted her, and sank his shaft into her willing pussy. Her slit-hole, creamed with the juices of desire, parted, and he slid deep into the bubbling heat of her cunt. She gasped and held on to his shoulders as he drove to the limit, burying his cock clear to the scrotum.

Laura Lee was wild. She bucked and thrashed like a colt on a winter morning. The harder he drove, the more she took. The more she took, the more he gave her, until their bodies sleeked with sweat and they both puffed for oxygen. Raider held on as long as he could and then surrendered his seed, bursting inside her as she screamed in his ear. Her fingernails raked his back until tiny rivulets of blood coursed down his sides, mingled with his perspiration.

She shuddered with the last spasms of orgasmic convulsions.

Raider fell on her, sated with her sex, the driving thrash of her loins and legs.

"You're some woman," he admitted. "Too damned good to be a whore."

She sighed and ran a finger through a damp curl of his hair that had fallen onto his forehead.

"I want to be the best there is," she said. "But I want to be my own woman."

"I know what you mean," he said. "What would happen if you just rode out of here?"

"Big Jake would either bring me back or kill me."

"Why do you say that?"

"Wanda. Everyone else thinks she's dead. Before she left, she promised to send back word that she was free. We've never heard anything since."

"Maybe she changed her mind."

"Not Wanda. She said she would send word by one of the freighters who brings in goods from Santa Fe. If she got that far."

"And she never did?"

Laura Lee shook her head and her eyes filled with tears. When he took her in his arms again she was trembling.

"I'll help you," he said. "But first you've got to help me. I want to know everything you know about Big Jake. Who his close friends are, the dates he's been gone, and where he's getting the silver for those Pecos dollars."

"For one thing," she said, "I lied to you."

He pushed her to arm's length, looked at her.

"About what?"

"About being a whore. I am, but not in the real sense. The only man I've known is Big Jake, and if he knew I was with you like this he'd kill me. He'd kill us both."

Raider swallowed something distasteful.

"Hell, everyone saw you come to my room."

"I know. But I knew you were the man to help me. And Big Jake taught me how to please a man."

"That's just fine, Laura Lee. Now I'm a marked man."

"You were the moment you rode into town. You're Raider, aren't you? That's all Big Jake has talked about lately. Raider and a man named Doc."

"Son of a bitch," he said softly. "Then what about that Burnett?"

"He just wanted to make sure."

"But he's not sure."

"He's sure by now. Big Jake has drawings of both of you. He got them from someone. Recently."

Raider felt like he was suffocating.

Suddenly the room got very small.

"What about the other part? You really want to run away from him?"

"That part is true. You're my only chance."

But he knew that she had probably fixed it so he couldn't help anyone. From now on he'd have to have eyes in the back of his head. And somehow he'd have to warn Doc.

"Why didn't Big Jake come after you now?" he asked.

"Because he's in Santa Fe and won't be back for another three days."

Raider let out a breath of relief.

Three days. Not much time. But right now, after what Laura Lee had told him, it seemed like a lifetime.

CHAPTER TWELVE

The Studebaker jolted to a halt.

Doc slid his derby back so he could see the rider approaching at a fast pace. Spooner was asleep in the back. The sun was only three hours old, at his back. He had been driving Judith since dawn, hoping to make Pecos Gulch by noon. Now he could smell the river. He pulled out a cheroot and struck a sulphur match on the butt of his Diamondback .38. He made sure his coat stayed back, in case he needed to draw the pistol.

He didn't recognize the horse, a blue roan, but the rider was unmistakable.

Raider rode up a few seconds later, a gunnysack tied to his saddle horn.

"This an official welcome?" said Doc. There was a stirring in the back of the wagon as Spooner began to wake up.

"Consider it that. What kept you?"

"I'm only half a day late. You get in last night?"

"I did. Had to sneak out before dawn this morning."

"Sneak out?"

Raider swung down, carefully avoiding the gunnysack. Still, he brushed against it. A whirring sound made the hackles rise on the back of Doc's neck.

"Yeah," said Raider, ground-tying the roan. "Seems Big Jake knows we're coming and we aren't supposed to leave without his permission."

Doc blew a flume of smoke into the dry air.

"What's that you have in the sack?"

"A little surprise. Want to put it in your carpetbags."

"Sounded like a rattlesnake to me."

"Sidewinder. I caught him a few minutes ago. He hasn't eaten, and he was stalking a kangaroo rat when I put a forked stick to the back of his head."

Doc held on to the side of the wagon. It shook as Spooner stood up in a crouching position and stuck his head out the front of the canvas opening.

"Who you got there? A pilgrim?"

"Be polite, Raider. Winton Spooner here grew up with Bill Pinkerton. He's on the case."

Raider looked him over, then cocked his head skeptically.

"He's a Pinkerton?"

Spooner climbed onto the seat and rubbed his eyes.

"No," said Doc. "He's a geologist."

"A rockhound."

Spooner laughed at Raider's comment.

"He's an expert on silver mines," said Doc.

"Throw down your carpetbag, Doc," said Raider.

"You're not putting a sidewinder in my bag."

"It's not for you." Raider told him about Burnett going through his saddlebags. "I'd like to give him a little surprise. Put him on edge."

"He might get bit," said Doc.

"Yeah, he might at that."

Raider loaded the rattlesnake into the carpetbag after Doc removed his journal and other personal items that he wouldn't need for a while. The snake thrashed around and then was quiet. Spooner watched in fascination, observing Raider with keen interest. He listened raptly as Raider explained the situation in Pecos Gulch. Raider spoke quickly and didn't waste time on explaining the import of what he had to say. Doc's eyebrows went up when Janet Logan's name was mentioned and when Raider explained that Big Jake Logan was probably her father. Doc didn't seem surprised when offered a description of the man who owned the town.

Spooner didn't say much, but it was apparent to Doc that he was enjoying himself. The only thing that worried Weatherbee was that the geologist seemed not to realize that he was on a dangerous assignment. When Raider remounted the blue roan and rode west, Doc laid down the ground rules for his companion.

"When we get to Pecos Gulch, you'd best stay to yourself. I'll get you a room and contact you when I need you. As far as anyone is concerned, you're just another prospector. You rode in with me, but we don't know each other. Clear?"

"I understand."

"From what Raider said, we're no longer undercover. Loman and the others there are expecting us. So we'll be targets. No use in your being one too."

"That Raider. It's hard to think of him working for Bill Pinkerton. Bill is so careful about...about people."

Doc looked at the geologist and stubbed out his cheroot. It was time to go. Raider had been gone long enough to give him a good lead. They were less than an hour from the town.

"Raider is a good operative. The Pinkerton Agency doesn't understand the West. They understand crime and good detection methods. If William or his brother were to come out here and act the way they do, they would be spotted immediately. Raider fits in. He's rough, he's crude, and he's hard as a boot. Beyond that, he's smart, in his own native way, and while I don't get along with him very well, I'd rather have him beside me in a fight than any man I know."

"And how does he feel about you, this Raider fellow?" asked Spooner.

"Personally, I think he hates my guts."

Spooner took up lodgings in a ramshackle miners' hotel called the Pecos Hotel while Doc put up his wagon in the livery. He left his journal carefully hidden in the false bottom and saw to it that Judith was grained and curried. He winced at the prices, but at least he had money, now that his reimbursements for expenses had caught up to him. He carried the carpetbag with him, holding it well away from his leg, as he trudged up to the Silver Dollar Hotel. Men snickered as he passed by, and he doffed his derby to a couple of ladies of the night who nodded to him, then giggled when he acknowledged them.

He checked in and was given a room down the hall from Raider's. He washed up, dusted off his clothes, and left his carpetbag in the middle of the bed, tightly closed.

At the saloon, Burnett saw him come in and take a table. Doc noted the man leave quickly after his arrival. He ordered a drink from one of the waiters. The place was crowded at lunchtime, and he was not suprised when Raider left the bar and came over and sat down. As they drank, Raider quickly filled Doc in on everything that had happened, leaving out the part about going to bed with Laura Lee Hope. He did mention that she was Big Jake's girl, though, and that Loman and Logan were probably one and the same man.

"Did you meet Janet's father?"

"No, we only corresponded. Pretty good cover, now that I think of it. An itinerant preacher would be able to travel without suspicion. If Loman is Janet's father, it puts a whole new light on the robbery."

"You think she was part of it."

"Maybe. Unwittingly, perhaps." The waiter dropped a slate off at the table with the bill of fare chalked in. Doc and Raider both drank lukewarm beer from a pail. It was early in the day yet.

The menu was simple: roast beef, beans, tortillas, stewed tomatoes.

"I could eat the south end of a northbound horse," said Raider.

"That may be what you're getting," commented Weatherbee wryly.

They ordered two lunches, more beer.

"Any sign of Lorelei Standish? Or Grabowski, Metz?" Raider shook his head.

"You say Loman's in Santa Fe. Could be he's bringing his daughter out."

"I thought of that, Doc. I hate to think of a sweet young

thing like that mixed up in this."

"This Loman or Logan, whoever he is, appears to have laid his groundwork well. The man has patience and organizing abilities. He must have thought things out pretty thoroughly."

"Hard to sit on a hundred thousand in silver for two years."

"That's another thing bothering me. I haven't said anything to Wagner yet, because I wasn't sure. But after seeing Pecos Gulch, what little of it there is, I'm even more convinced that there's more to that robbery than meets the eye. If four or five men pulled it off and spent their ill-gotten gains on wine, women, and song, that's one thing. But instead they sat on the silver dollars and then went to a lot of trouble melting them down and stamping out Pecos dollars. That's expensive. This whole operation is expensive."

"What're you getting at, Doc?"

Before he could reply they heard a wild yell from upstairs in the hotel. Then two shots spaced together. Then another. Men in the saloon froze. It grew quiet.

Raider looked at Doc and grinned.

"That would be Burnett," he said.

"There'll be hell to pay."

"The only reason no one's braced us yet is because Big Jake's out of town. They know who we are, Doc. They've been waiting for us."

The waiter brought the two meals and set the plates down on the table with a clatter. The steaks were thin, charred almost black. He gave them forks.

"You'll have to use your own knives on that meat," he said.

"The cook fall asleep?" asked Raider.

"Sir?"

"You got charcoal here."

"He cooks everything well-done."

Weatherbee laughed and began scraping soot off his steak. The food was hot, anyway, and the two men wolfed down their meal. Weatherbee used Raider's knife on his steak.

The centers of the meat were red, the beef tough as buffalo hide.

All eyes turned when Burnett came downstairs and stalked into the saloon.

His left hand was wrapped in a bandanna. He carried a pistol in his right hand. Draped over the barrel was a headless sidewinner rattlesnake.

"Uh oh," said Raider. "Here he comes."

Burnett walked straight toward the Pinkerton's table. Raider's right hand slid down to his pistol butt.

The men in the room cleared a path. Another silence welled up as knives and forks hung motionless in midair and drinks stopped halfway to men's lips.

The gunman stopped at the table where Raider and Doc sat.

With a flick of his gun barrel he flipped the snake onto the table.

"Not so damned funny," snarled Burnett.

"I beg your pardon," said Doc.

"Think you're pretty smart, don't you? Mister, if I get real sick from snakebite, I'm going to blow your head off just like I did that sidewinder there."

Burnett lifted the pistol and aimed it at Weatherbee's head.

From underneath the table came the sound of an audible *click*. Burnett's thumb, on the hammer of his pistol, twitched. He did not cock the hammer back on the single-action Colt Peacemaker. Instead, his gaze shifted to Raider.

Raider's eyes narrowed.

"You even twitch, you son of a bitch," said the operative, "and you'll have the worst stomachache in your short life."

Burnett's face paled as it drained of color.

The bandanna fell off his left hand. A man nearby sucked in his breath. Another, seeing the wound, gasped.

The hardcase had tied a tourniquet just above his wrist. Where the rattler had bitten him he had slashed an X with his knife. The slashes were deep. The wound was runny with pus and venom and blood.

"Likely you'll live," said Doc evenly, "if you don't move around much and keep that tourniquet on. Loosen it every half hour slightly, and keep your hand down to let the venom drain. If you like, I've got some elixir in my wagon that will help alleviate the symptoms."

"Huh?" asked Burnett.

"I'm a doctor," said Weatherbee. "I sell medicine."

"You're a damned—"

Raider cut him off.

"Put your iron away, Burnett," he said, "slow and easy. I've got a hair trigger on this pistol, and my finger's inside the guard. If I so much as sneeze, this Remington's going to go off."

Burnett let his hand fall. He holstered his Colt, with its pitted barrel, the bluing worn away so that it was a dull gray. He let his left hand hang down straight, as Doc had advised him.

"You ain't gettin' away with this," he said to Weather-bee.

"Why, I don't know what you mean, sir. If you got bit by this snake, why bother me about it? You weren't illegally in my room, were you? I *have* kept a snake or two for medicinal purposes. The venom is used in several medicants very effectively. If I were you, I'd keep that in mind. You never know where a poisonous serpent might turn up."

Raider eased the hammer back down on his Remington .44. He made no sound and kept the pistol leveled at Burnett's gut.

The veins in Burnett's neck bulged, the blood so close to the surface it ran blue welts. He clenched his fists as if to quell his anger. Doc's eyes stayed wide. Raider kept his thumb snug on the hammer of his pistol.

"You'd better take care of that bite, one way or the other," said Raider. "If you see red streaks going up your arm, you better cut it off or say your prayers."

"You bastards," Burnett hissed. "I'll get your asses for this."

"Why, sir, you couldn't possibly be threatening us?" said

Doc. "Blaming us for something we didn't do. If a man keeps a snake among his goods, that's his business. If a thief sticks his hand in a man's personal valise and gets hurt, he surely can't blame the owner of the luggage."

"You calling me a thief?" muttered Burnett, halfheartedly. He looked at this arm as if to check on the streaks that Raider had mentioned.

"Did you take anything besides that snake here?"

"Fuck you."

"My, such crude talk for a man who might be facing his maker. I suggest you heed my friend's words. You may be, at this moment, dying of poison. If that snake venom hits your heart, you'll gasp for breath, you'll feel like you have ropes around your chest. Your face will turn purple, and you'll..."

Burnett paled and walked way. He knocked a man sideways who got in his way. By the time he reached the door to the hotel lobby, he was loping.

Doc laughed low.

Raider slid his pistol back in its holster.

The laughter spread, became a roar. Men came up and slapped Doc on the back. They eyed Raider warily, because some had seen his pistol slick out smooth from its holster. But Doc seemed the friendly one, the one most likely to appreciate their gestures of goodwill. Drinks were ordered up, and a piano player tinkled out a lively tune. The tension drifted away, although some had wanted blood. The dead snake was passed from hand to hand, and most agreed that they had been witness to an event that could be passed along, spoken about over late-night campfires or in trail towns somewhere down the road.

"I'm turning in," said Raider after he'd drunk a third free drink. "You staying?"

Doc smiled.

"Yes," he said. "I'm enjoying this brief moment in the limelight. Besides, I sense there may be need of powerful elixirs among the sad brethren of Pecos Gulch. Balms of Gilead for the masses."

"Weatherbee, you're full of shit. All kinds of shit."

"Good night, Raider. Even your sarcasm cannot dampen my exhilaration."

Raider stalked off through the crowd. Men parted to give him room, then crowded around Weatherbee to ask him questions.

One man, a grizzled miner called Two Fingers because he had that many digits on one hand, with three stumps in place of missing ones, spoke to Doc when the crowd began to thin.

"Don't mind me butting in," said he, "but Burnett won't forget what you and the quiet one did to him. Yessir, you got big troubles here in the Gulch."

Doc regarded the man with interest.

"And do you not have troubles here?"

"Some. They say there's silver here, a lode. But I've been digging in hard rock for thirty years and I don't see anything. Ought to be here, but I ain't seed doodly."

"Good point." Doc introduced himself and learned the man's handle. "But Big Jake has a mine."

"Has one, and we see his silver. But nobody can stake out close to it. His cronies have claims all around it."

"You think he's found silver, Two Fingers?"

The old man scratched his head. He was slope-shouldered, had most of his hair, and was almost as broad as he was tall. Small, off-center eyes bracketed a nose that was as flat as a flapjack and spread out over a fifth of his face. His smile revealed dark and scraggly teeth with gaps in between like the missing slats in a ramshackle picket fence.

"Don't rightly know. Could be. That's what they say, like I told you. A big hole there. Might be deep. Ought to be silver here. Gold, too, maybe."

"But you're not sure."

Two Fingers shook his head.

"What's sure? But I can smell silver."

"And do you smell silver here?"

"I smell a lot of it, Doc, but it don't smell good."

CHAPTER THIRTEEN

Winton Spooner didn't like it.

Doc wanted to strangle him, but he kept his baser emotions in check.

Two Fingers didn't give a damn one way or another. Weatherbee's twenty-dollar gold piece was the first hard money he'd had in ten weeks that was above the denomination of six bits silver.

"Spooner, this is not your usual survey job. You weren't hired to roam around and spot geological formations."

"But I'm a geologist."

"And I sell snake oil. We're after one specific place. A so-called silver mine. Two Fingers here is going to help us find it. I want you to check it out, see if it really is a producing silver mine. Can you do that?"

"Well, I...I've been down in mines before, and I can surely tell if—"

"Fine, fine. Trust me. I need two things right away. Two Fingers is going to show you where the mine is located. Go there. Check it out. Then I want to set up my camera and take pictures."

"Outside or in?"

Doc grimaced.

"Outside is fine for now. It's hard enough to photograph in good daylight without going down into a pit in this godforsaken country. We don't have much time. Loman will be back in town tomorrow or the next day."

"Might be trouble," said the laconic Two Fingers.

Doc turned and thought about strangling him, too. It was early in the morning, and he'd spent a long time talking to the old miner, setting this all up the evening before. Two

Fingers, who would not give him any other name, had been wary of him. In certain places the Pinkerton name was not an invitation to a lasting friendship.

"Why?" he asked, patiently. "Is the mine guarded?"

"Sure is," said Two Fingers. "I don't think we can get within five hundred yards of that hole in the hillside."

"Well, that's Spooner's job. I'll come up with my medicine wagon after he's had a look at it and bluff my way through."

"All right," said Spooner. "But I don't guarantee much under these conditions. In fact, I can't guarantee anything."

"Just tell me if you think there's a producing silver mine anywhere in this gulch."

Spooner scratched his head, then agreed to go with Two Fingers. The unlikely pair set off on horseback several minutes later. Doc left to get Raider up and ready the medicine wagon for a trip to the "silver mine." Few people were about at that hour, and he was not detained.

"We have a problem, Raider," said Doc.

Raider dressed while Weatherbee talked.

"What else is new?"

"I mean, we're on our own here for a time. There's no telegraph here. Nearest place is Pecos, or Santa Fe."

"What difference does it make? Wagner wouldn't understand this situation anyway."

"I keep wondering how far a hundred dollars would stretch. I made all the saloons, gambling dens, and whorehouses with a man named Two Fingers last night. The town is making money, but there's grumbling among the miners. The payroll has got to be high. Question is, is there enough money coming in for Big Jake to make a profit, or is this whole thing just a sham?"

Raider pulled on his boots. He had scraped his beard with cold water and an even colder straight razor. There were little drops of blood on his face where he had shaved too close.

"I don't get you, Doc."

Doc bit the end off a cheroot but did not light it. Instead

he twirled and rolled it in his hands as he thought out loud.

"Let's say that Loman or Logan planned the robbery for a long time. Then he made his move. He had to have inside help, knowledge of that special shipment. Abernathy might have been the key man there, as you think he was. If he's not dead, then that's strong evidence that he was in on this from the beginning. And then we find that Janet Logan is not what she seemed. She is the daughter of the bandits' leader. We have two mint employees in on the robbery, perhaps. Grabowski and Lorelei Standish. And there's an ex-mint employee, the engraver, Metz. Follow me so far?"

Raider slipped his gunbelt around his waist and cinched it up. He strode to the table and sat down.

"Almost looks as if everyone involved worked for the mint at one time or another."

"Exactly!" exclaimed Weatherbee.

"But there were others involved in the actual robbery that we can't identify. The bald-headed man is probably Grabowski. The short man must be Metz. Who's the tall man? Abernathy? And the man with the limp? The big man? Big Jake?"

"Anyone can fake a limp. Burnett could have been that man. We'll know if Big Jake fits the description of the big man when we see him. But I saw someone last night I want you to check out. Could be the tall man."

"Yeah?"

"Only it's not a man."

"Not a man?"

"Lorelei Standish. Tallest woman I ever saw. Over six foot, I'd say."

"Abernathy's tall too."

"But a killer? I doubt it. Wait until you see Miss Standish."

"Where'd you find her?"

"The Pleasure Palace. You'll enjoy yourself."

"She's a whore?"

"She's the madam. I didn't go in. Saw her through the window. Some pretty attractive ladies in the parlor. They

looked like midgets next to her. And she looks tough enough
to put a man down."

"I don't like messing with a woman."

Doc got up, shoved the cheroot in his mouth, and looked
for a match in his vest pockets.

"Part of the job, Raider. See you tonight."

"Where?"

"At the Pleasure Palace."

"You bastard."

Doc smiled, tipped his hat.

And then he was gone.

Spooner and Two Fingers were waiting for Weatherbee
when he drove the wagon to the edge of town. Doc knew
the general direction of the silver mine from Two Fingers'
account of the night before. At first he was disappointed
that the two men were waiting for him. He thought, mis-
takenly, that this meant they had failed.

"The mine is well located," said Spooner, assuaging Doc's
doubts before he had even set the brake. "Assuming there
are silver deposits of quantity in these hills."

"How close did you get?" asked Doc.

"Close enough," said Two Fingers. "There's only two
guards, and I know both of them. Did some trading." He
held up a bottle of whiskey which was almost empty. The
miner's breath reeked of whiskey. Spooner stood well away
from him, closer to the two mules they had ridden to the
mine.

"I was able to examine the terrain. Mine's located at a
juncture between two low hills. I guess you'd call it an
arroyo."

"Blind arroyo," said Two Fingers. "Runs downhill from
the mine, though, so there's no drain-off into the hole."

"Can we get close enough to take a photograph?" asked
Doc.

"I think so," said Spooner. "Both of the guards are three
sheets to the wind if they're still standing up. I took ore
samples from around the mine. Won't tell us much, though.

If there is a vein, it could be deep. In fact, it probably is. The hills here don't indicate any silver deposits close to the surface."

"You can tell that just from looking?"

"Pretty much. But there's another reason I say that if they're getting silver out of that hole they're going deep."

"All right," said Doc. "How do you know that?"

"Few tailings. Just a trace around the mine."

Doc drew a breath. "That's important?"

"I'd say so, yes. If they went straight in and found enough silver ore to mine there'd be more tailings. I asked Two Fingers here to bring me back some tailings. I've got them in my bag. Tonight I'll run tests on them. If there is silver in there, I should find traces in that blasted rock."

"I see," said Doc. He was in way over his head and knew it. He told them to lead him to the mine. He was already figuring how to photograph it. He wouldn't use the Premo Sr. camera but a box of Rockwood's design that would take an image on the 8/10 plate. It would be tricky, but he'd have a large photograph that would take in a large area and show exact detail concerning the location of the mine. The developing would be the hard part, under the worst conditions outside of a studio. But he had all the chemicals, and if he could get his room dark enough it might work. Wagner wanted hard evidence on this one; he meant to leave no rough edges.

Raider spent most of the day exploring the town. This was not idle curiosity on his part, but investigative work. He looked for buildings large enough to house a minting operation. He found three buildings large enough to contain the equipment necessary to melt down silver coins and make new ones. He checked out each one. The first building served as a warehouse for mercantile goods. The second stored a jumble of equipment: tools, dynamite, paint, lumber, harness and tack, wagons—things necessary to build a town.

The third building, like the others, had a chimney, but

a much larger one that was really three chimneys in one. It was guarded by two men.

One man sat at the front entrance under a wooden lean-to. The other circled the building. Both men had rifles and pistols. The walking guard carried a Winchester '73 cradled in his arms and smoked constantly. The guard under the lean-to braided a rope out of hemp strands. He was very patient, but he concentrated more on his braiding than on looking around him. That was why Raider was able to stand in the shadows between two buildings and observe the two men without being seen.

The walking guard drank from a wooden canteen every so often. He left his post to piss on a rock in a clump of cactus twice within an hour's time. He would spend two or three minutes talking to the rope maker on each of his rounds.

There was no sound coming from the building.

Raider watched them for two hours, then took a break. He watched them for another hour, paying careful attention to their routine.

The building was the farthest out from town, isolated from the nearest one, where Raider stood, by close to a hundred yards. It was hot, even in the shade, and Raider sweated. But he made no noise, and he kept himself well tucked back in the shadows. Late in the afternoon two men walked up and relieved the other guards. The rope maker had completed some twenty feet of rope. He coiled it, wrapped the loose strands, and lugged it off over his shoulder. The walking guard said something to his relief that Raider couldn't hear. The shadows told him it was about four o'clock in the afternoon when the guard changed.

And in another few hours it would be dark. That was probably when still another shift came on. Say, eight o'clock. He would check again. He watched the second pair of guards for an hour. These two didn't say much. The sitter whittled on a small block of wood. The walker didn't stay so close to the building, but made a wider swing. Every so often he would go to high ground. This would be one to watch. He was restless, nervous. Every so often he would look in Raider's direction and hold his gaze for a long time as if trying to see into the deepening shadows. Raider never made a move, but he had an eerie feeling that the man knew he was there.

When he left to go back to the hotel, he swung by the Pleasure Palace. It was quiet at that hour, but he saw a curtain move upstairs. The bawdy house was at the end of the main street. It sported a tall false front that had been decorated with paintings of half-nude women in provocative poses. Big-hipped women with veils and nymph-like women with tiny fans held coyly over their private parts. The sign above the pictures of cavorting women called the establishment MADAME LORELEI'S PLEASURE PALACE.

Raider hitched his belt as he walked back to the hotel.

He hoped the place lived up to its name.

After standing for hours, he was ready to mix a little pleasure with business.

Doc made arrangements to meet Spooner later in the evening, after the geologist had gone over the ore samples he had collected. During the time he was taking his careful photographs, Spooner gathered more tailings from around the mine entrance and went over the surrounding country with a pick and sack, studying the rocks and the earth. He would not commit himself, but told Doc that he would try, in the next few days, to enter the mine itself.

"Fair enough," said Doc. "But be careful. Check with me before you do."

The men split up, with Two Fingers and Spooner returning to town together, while Doc babied the Studebaker back to the livery. He had carefully packed the exposed 8 × 10 glass plates in dust-proof boxes, each plate fitted into a tight wooden slot so that it was set rigidly in place. The boxes were then put in a large box that was packed with crystals of dry ice he had kept packed in the heavy duck canvas. The boxes rested in a sling he had constructed inside the wagon so that they would not be jarred while traveling over the rough road. He held Judith to a walk in order to further insure that he would not damage the exposed plates before he had the chance to develop them.

Back in his room, Weatherbee made notes in his journal while waiting for dark. He wrote swiftly, carefully, theorizing in between layers of fact. When he was finished, the sun had gone down over the western hills and darkness had settled over Pecos Gulch. Doc stripped his bed, sealed off the crack under the door with a blanket, pulled all the shades, and used the sheets to seal off other apertures where light might seep through. He set out his trays and chemicals and replaced the chimney lamp with one that had been specially coated with lampblack and thick yellow paint. The faint glow from the modified lamp gave Doc enough light to see but was not enough to damage the exposed plates.

When he had all his equipment set up, Doc slid open the ends of a box containing the glass plates and gingerly lifted the first plate out. He had coated all the plates that day delicately with collodion. The collodion was "carried" in solution with the excitants Doc used, in this case bromide and iodide of potassium. When he had finished coating the plate, he had let the ether and alcohol evaporate to just the right degree of stickiness before lowering it into a deep "bath holder" which contained a solution of nitrate of silver.

The solution worked fine in the field at about 60 degrees Fahrenheit. This operation made the plate sensitive, and had to be done in total darkness except for the same subdued yellow light he used now. Doc had sealed the inside of the wagon with heavy duck canvas and worked under a photographer's black shroud. After allowing the plate to "coat" for about five minutes, he had put the plate into a slide, or holder, and had then taken his camera to its tripod to take the photograph. The life of a wet plate, except during cold weather, was not more than an hour on either side of the exposure, either the coating or development side, and usually had to be developed within a few minutes following exposure, but new techniques and chemicals had extended the life of the plate. But now Doc worked fast. Every moment of delay resulted in a loss of brilliancy and depth in the negative.

The coolness, the care he had taken, and the delicate mix of chemicals produced sharp negatives. Doc was pleased. He finished developing the exposed plates, printed out one for a sample, then packed everything away. The negatives were put back in their boxes. He carried his equipment back to the livery, stored it all on cushions in the false bottom, and locked it all up. It was late. He was hungry and thirsty. By now Raider ought to be at the Pleasure Palace, and Doc had no intention of letting his partner have all the fun.

He had seen a couple of pretties the night before, and the thought of them now made him forget about his hunger pangs.

He set out along the main street for the Pleasure Palace.

Before he had gone twenty paces from the livery, he heard his name called.

He turned and saw a man step off the boardwalk halfway down the street. The man, shrouded in shadow, was unrecognizable. As the man started toward him, gunfire erupted from two or three different directions. Orange flame and white smoke punctuated the darkness. Bullets whistled in the air. Doc heard a ball sizzle close to his ear.

He dove for the ground, clawing for his pistol.

CHAPTER FOURTEEN

Doc landed on the street with a *whump*, knocking the air from his lungs.

A bullet plowed a furrow inches from his face, stinging his eyes with grit. His fingers fumbled for the Diamondback .38 riding high on his belt in its holster.

The man who had hailed him staggered a few feet and twitched as a pistol roared and a bullet struck him low in the hip.

Doc jerked the revolver clear of its holster and rolled toward the safety of a watering trough.

A flash of orange flame spewed from between two buildings. Doc swung his pistol to home in on the target and fired at the cloud of white smoke that lingered. His ears throbbed with the sounds of the explosions. He heard a man cry out. Another man cursed. Two shots rang out, and bullets ripped into the wooden trough, gouging .45-caliber holes in the sides. Wood splintered into spears and flew in all directions. Weatherbee hugged the ground.

As quickly as it had started, it was over. He heard a sound like a man being dragged away. Muffled voices faded into silence.

The man who had been shot was down when Doc got to his feet.

Cautiously, he approached him, the .38 still in his hand, his finger on the trigger.

The man groaned.

Doc stood above him for a few seconds, looking all around.

The bushwhackers had gone.

Weatherbee knelt down and touched the man's back.

There were at least three bullet holes visible in the dim light from a street lantern hung on a post. He turned the man over as gently as he could and tried to make out his face.

It was Two Fingers.

He was alive.

Just barely.

"Doc?" croaked the miner.

"Yes. I'm here. Know who shot you?"

"Jess Burnett. Merle Jenkins."

"There were three of them after you."

"Got me bad, huh?"

Doc looked down at Two Fingers' chest and legs. There was blood soaked through his trousers at his thigh. So much blood he couldn't see the hole. If it was an exit wound, it would be big enough. It the ball had smashed an artery, the miner would be dead in a few minutes. There was blood on his stomach, high on his chest. Higher than the heart, but high enough to tear some lung.

"I probably could tie off your leg, give you a few minutes."

"It hurts bad, Doc. Especially here." He coughed and pointed to his belly. The blood was bubbling there, bubbling with every pulsebeat. No way to stop it. If an artery had been hit, it was somewhere inside him. The poor bastard was probably filling up with blood. Drowning in it.

"Why were they after you?"

"Saw me and you today. They worked me over first."

Doc looked closely. He laid his pistol in the dirt next to Two Fingers and lit a match. The miner's face was bruised, welted. The skin over one cheekbone was crushed. One eye was almost closed. The lids shone an ugly purple in the matchlight. Doc winced and blew out the flame.

"There were three shooting at you. I couldn't see them."

"Just two. Burnett and Jenkins. Merle's a mean little bastard. Forgot about him. If there was three, it had to be her. Merle's boss. He works at . . ."

Two Fingers coughed, choked. His eyes closed, and Doc

thought he was gone. But they opened again, and he moved his mouth to speak.

Nothing came out.

"Hold on. Is there a real doctor in town?"

"Aren't you . . . ?"

That was all he said. He gave a sigh, and something terrible rattled in his throat. His head fell back on the dirt, and he stared sightless at the dark, star-stippled sky.

"No, Two Fingers," whispered Doc. "I'm not."

He stood up and holstered his pistol with an angry shove.

Doc walked up the street, brushing the dust off his clothes. A muscle twitched in his jaw.

Two Fingers hadn't deserved to die. Not like that. Without a chance, gunned down in the street. Shot in the back. The Pinkerton Agency would have to pay for his burial. To hell with them and their damned miserly overseeing of expenses.

It was too bad the dying miner hadn't been able to finish what he had been trying to say. Merle worked for a man who might have been the other killer. Doc was sure there had been three men shooting at him and Two Fingers. The crossfire had been deadly. The miner hadn't had a chance.

Who was the third man, then?

It was too bad that Jess Burnett had survived the snakebite. Or maybe it was better that he had. He would know who the other man was. So would Jenkins. Merle Jenkins.

Doc vowed to remember the name. He vowed, too, to find him and make him talk.

He walked rapidly toward the Pleasure Palace, but he had a queasy feeling in the pit of his stomach.

Two Fingers had been killed because he had been seen with a Pinkerton.

If *he* had been seen, then so had Spooner.

Raider grinned at the pretty girl with the tray.

"What you got there?" he asked.

"Brandy. On the house."

"Brandy, or that foul Mexican *aguardiente* that tastes like horse piss?"

The girl laughed.

"This is good brandy."

Raider took a shot glass from the tray and downed its contents. The alcohol burned all the way down, then turned his stomach mellow. He grinned again and gazed down at the girl's breast. The cleavage of her bodice was severe. He could see almost to her navel. Her breasts were handfuls, and he was tempted. Mighty tempted.

"Not bad," he said, wiping his lips with the back of his hand.   .

"You mean the brandy or my tits?"

He laughed self-consciously.

"Hey, you got a sense o' humor."

"That's not all I've got," she teased.

"What's your name, honey?"

"It's not honey. Alice."

"Alice Fewclothes?"

She laughed.

"Alice Cummings. Not that it matters. You're new here in the Gulch."

"Hell, Alice, I'm new most everywhere. You just serve drinks, or do you play?"

She glided away.

"I do a lot of things," she said. "Make yourself to home."

Alice was blonde, blue-eyed, young. She was not tall, but her proportions made her seem taller than she was. She wore net stockings and a short skirt of black taffeta that made noises when she walked. Her legs were good. Raider saw only one bruise that was big enough and black enough to show through the powder she had dabbed on the plump part of her leg just beneath her left buttock. Her face was round and comely, the eyebrows heavy, her eyelashes long. Her eyes were sad, though, despite her banter and her seemingly spontaneous laughter.

Not a happy woman. The eyes were haunted. She looked like a young doe in the woods about to break from cover.

He read fear in her eyes, and defeat, as if she had been broken to submission against her will. But he was wary, after Laura Lee.

Besides, he had not come there to dally with the help.

He was after the boss.

Lorelei Standish.

He took a seat on the divan. The parlor was plush—gawdy, even. There was a wide beaded doorway beyond. He could see part of the stairway and a table that held a vase with wildflowers of gold and blue and red. Men sat in corners with drinks and had their hands up between the legs of the women who sat opposite them. A man and woman were kissing on a love seat, and their legs were entwined and tangled, so that they looked like a couple of broken mannequins in a store window.

A small dark girl looked at Raider, then turned away. She picked up a snuff box from her lap and sniffed the fine powder into her nostrils. She shook her head and held her finger up to her nose to keep from sneezing. Raider could see up between her thighs, under the skirt, to the dark thatch of pubic hairs that bearded her sex. She wore very thin pink panties that fit tightly, like skin.

There was a small bar, tended by a burly, pugnacious man who seemed to double as a bouncer. He had heavy sloping shoulders and a blunt, bullet-shaped head. It took Raider several seconds to realize that the man was wearing a toupee. The hairline didn't quite match up. The man's eyebrows were light blond; the hairpiece was dark brown.

Unless he missed his guess, the man behind the bar was Grabowski.

Before he could check that assumption out, a shadow fell across him as someone walked up and blocked out the light.

Raider looked up. And up.

She was tall. Over six feet in her high-heeled shoes. She wore a skirt that was slit down one side, exposing a graceful leg. Her eyes were blue, her hair champagne, curly. She was wide-shouldered, with a haughty grace that was patrician, intimidating. Her nose was straight, slightly hooked at the end. She had full lips, and white, even teeth when she smiled.

She smiled now. And spoke.

"Is someone helping you, mister? Do you see anyone you like?"

"No. And yes."

"Oh? You've found a girl?"

Raider stood up and took off his hat. He looked straight into Lorelei Standish's eyes. Her smile faded, and her lips twisted into a wry, mocking shape. Her blue eyes turned cold as ice. Raider felt the sudden chill.

"Yes," he said. "You."

"I'm sorry, but I run the Palace. I'm not available for your pleasure. And I didn't get your name."

"Raider."

Her eyes flickered, but she didn't move. Nor did her face change expression.

"The Pinkerton."

"Does that make any difference?"

"It does here." Her gaze drifted to the bartender. Raider watched him out of the corner of his eye.

"Can we talk? Privately."

"We can talk. Are you here for business or pleasure?"

"Tonight, strictly for pleasure."

"Perhaps one of the girls..."

"No, Miss Standish, not one of the girls. You." His voice was pitched low; it did not carry beyond the two of them.

"I've told you, that's out of the question."

"Is it?"

She looked over at the bewigged bartender again.

"If that moose makes one move from behind the bar, I'll blow his fucking head off," Raider said softly, with a smile. "Wig and all."

A startled look widened Lorelei's eyes. She stepped back and looked Raider up and down.

The smile continued to play on his lips.

A change came over Lorelei. She stepped back close and touched his right arm at the biceps. Her long fingers played over the muscle.

"I've heard you were tough," she said. "A hard man to get down."

"I'm easy," he said, his meaning clear.

"I like violent men. Tough men. Maybe we can talk some."

"In private?"

"I have a room in the back." She looked at the bartender, raised her voice. "It's all right, Ed. See that we're not disturbed."

Raider looked at Grabowski. The burly Pole frowned and folded his arms.

"What do you feed him?" Raider asked as she led him from the parlor to a hallway beyond the beaded curtain. "Raw wolf meat?"

Lorelei laughed. Her laughter was low-pitched, sensual. Despite himself, Raider felt his loins tug with desire. The madam's dress fit her like a glove. He could see the muscles of her buttocks ripple underneath the silk of her dress. And, too, there was that flashing bare leg, slipping in and out of the slit sheath.

The lamps were lit in her room, throwing a rosy light through the colored glass chimneys. The room was bathed in a crimson glow. The drapes were plush, the carpeting thick. All crimson. Even the flocked wallpaper was red velvet. The bedspread on the brass bed was pink with red tassel trim.

She shut the door after he entered and turned the key in the lock.

"Now we won't be disturbed," she said. "Would you like something to drink?"

"What are you having?"

"Brandy." She saw his look. "Santa Fe brandy. The best."

"You've lived well the past two years."

"I lived well before that."

She poured two brandy snifters half full, then handed him one.

"You worked at the Denver mint."

"I am sure you know most everything."

"No. I don't know why. Three men were killed that night, and a hundred thousand dollars doesn't stretch very far when it's split five or six ways."

Her eyebrows arched slightly. She sat on a small divan and crossed her legs so that the bare one showed. Like a beacon. Raider sailed his hat onto the bed and sat in a straight-backed chair next to a spindly-legged table. He set his drink on a crocheted doily.

"I could tell you everything, I suppose. It wouldn't do you any good. You'd just carry the information to your grave."

"An early grave?"

"Raider, you won't get out of the Gulch alive."

He felt the coldness of her words. She sat there, glacially seductive, that single bare leg dangling provocatively. It was the longest, prettiest leg he'd ever seen on a woman.

"You seem pretty sure of yourself."

"Big Jake will be here tomorrow. He's been waiting for you. The only reason you're alive now is that he wants to make you a proposition first."

"Oh? About what?"

"I have no idea. But I imagine there would be quite a bit of money involved. And perhaps a job of some sort. Big Jake thinks big. He's very persuasive."

"Did he draw you into this?"

She ignored the question and just sipped at her drink.

"You don't like the question," he said. A flat statement.

"I do what I want to do."

"Are you in love with Branfield Logan? Or Loman? Big Jake?"

It was a shot in the dark.

Her composure seemed to melt like candle wax. Her face contorted, and he could feel the rage seething from her. Her hand gripped the brandy snifter very tightly, as if she were considering either breaking it with her bare hand or throwing it at him. Then she drew herself up, relaxed.

"You're think you're smart," she said quietly. "But you don't really know very much. There's a lot more involved here than a mere robbery."

"More than the mere death of innocent men," he said, his eyes narrowing to accusing slits.

"Yes," she hissed. "Yes."

"I guess Laura Lee Hope beat you out," he said mercilessly.

"That bitch! Big Jake can't see through her like I can. But when he gets back and finds out she spread her legs for you, he'll throw her out like a used rag."

"She wants out."

"Oh? Did she tell you that?"

"She's ambitious. And good at her trade. Did you train her?"

Lorelei's lips pinched together and her eyes dulled— signs of bitter contemplation. The more he looked at her and listened to her, the more he realized how little he knew about her. Cold-blooded. Hard. Beautiful. Mysterious. Complex. Yes, all of those things. But he didn't know what made her tick. He didn't know why she had turned thief and killer and whore.

And he didn't know why she hated men.

CHAPTER FIFTEEN

By the time Doc reached the Pleasure Palace, word of the shooting had spread among the patrons and girls. When he went inside, the bartender wore a look of surprise on his face. The girl with the tray of drinks looked at him too, very closely. Her expression went blank and her skin drained of color.

As if she was looking at a ghost.

Weatherbee smiled at both of them, walked over to the girl, and lifted a brandy from the tray. He plunked a silver dollar down. It rattled noisily on the tray. The buzz of conversation rose and fell, and he knew that people were talking about Two Fingers lying out there on the empty street dead.

"Thank . . . thank you, sir," said Alice Cummings.

"You're a pretty little thing. Won't you join me?"

She looked at Grabowski. He nodded.

"Yes. Do you want to go upstairs?"

"Yes. A little privacy would be most conducive to my intentions."

She giggled nervously and set the tray down on the bar. Doc looked at the bartender closely.

"Your toupee is on crooked, Mr. Grabowski," he said congenially. "You may want to adjust it before it falls in one of the drinks."

Grabowski scowled.

"How'd you know my name?" he asked gruffly.

"Why, you're famous, my man."

"Famous?"

Doc offered Alice his arm, as a gentleman would. She took it, flattered.

"Of course," said Doc as Alice led him toward the beaded curtains and the stairs beyond. "There isn't a peace officer in the land who doesn't know your name by now."

Whatever Grabowski replied was unintelligible as Doc and the girl passed out of earshot.

"You shouldn't have said that to Ed," said Alice. "If you get him mad, no telling what he's liable to do."

"He been here all evening?"

"Yes." The stairs creaked as they made their way up to the landing. Alice held on to the railing and Doc's arm. "He generally is. He watches over Miss Lorelei."

"And where is she, my pretty?"

"With a man."

"Yes. But with whom?"

"I . . . I think he called himself Raider."

"Um, yes. Works fast, doesn't he?"

Alice opened the door to a room down the hall. Laughter and the creak of bedsprings sounded from other rooms. She closed the door and locked it. A single lamp spread a cone of light over the wall and ceiling. The room was feminine, though Spartan. Crude bed, frilly bedspread. Watercolors of naked women on the walls. A framed photograph of a man and woman engaged in coitus hung near the bed. The background was dark, the couple standing out in contrast with their white, naked bodies. The woman was beefy in the hips; the man was small, slender, hairy.

Alice began to undress.

Doc hung his hat on a tree and slipped out of his coat.

"That will be twenty dollars," she said. "In advance. My name is Alice, and for ten more dollars I'll do anything you want."

"Anything?"

"Most anything. Suck you. You can suck me."

"How crudely put."

"Most of the men who come here are crude," she said, without apology.

"You came of your own free will."

She looked at him sharply, turning so that he caught the

full brunt of her nakedness. She was beautiful. Shapely, with pert, upturned breasts, a softly rounded tummy. Not the usual plump whore with homely face and greasy hair.

"You think that?"

"Well, didn't you?" Doc continued to undress, now that he saw what he was getting for his twenty dollars.

"Mister, you don't look as dumb as you are. I was shanghaied—I think that's the term—by that bald-headed man down there and Big Jake."

Doc sat down and pulled off his boots. He skidded his trousers down his legs and folded them neatly before laying them over the back of the chair.

"Where'd they pick you up?"

"Santa Fe. I was looking for a ride to Fort Sumner. They said they were going that way. That was a month ago."

"You never did this before?"

"I didn't say that. I never did it for pay. I was a waitress."

"Looks like these boys are into a little white slavery to boot."

Doc went to her and smoothed her hair with his palm while he admired her body up close.

"Say, who are you anyway? The law?"

"Name's Doc Weatherbee. I'm a vendor of medicines."

"In a pig's eye. They've been talking of little else for weeks. You're a Pinkerton agent. A damned detective."

"Well, we call ourselves operatives. And we do some detecting. They say anything else?"

"No, they just expected you to show up sooner or later. I gather they don't mean to let you leave the Gulch alive."

"I suppose not. Shall we?" Doc waved a hand toward the bed.

"Did you forget the money? I don't want any trouble."

Doc walked back to the chair and took a twenty-dollar bill out of a money clip. He laid it on the dresser. Alice looked at it and climbed into bed.

"You want the lamp out?"

"No," he said. "And I don't want the extras. I'll provide those."

Doc caressed her until she was warm and he was hot. She spread her legs as he mounted her. He sank in deep. He stroked her slow, so slow that she began to squirm and writhe. He nudged up against her clit and rubbed it with his swollen cock until she jolted with a sudden orgasm.

"Lord!" she exclaimed. "I didn't expect that."

She shivered all over as if drenched with ice water.

Doc smiled cryptically and then did it to her again. This time Alice bucked as if electrocuted. Her fingernails dug into his back. Her legs flew up into the air spontaneously.

"Lord a-mighty!" she shrieked. "I ought to pay you, mister. I mean Doc."

"Yes," he said. "The thought has occurred to me more than once that I missed my calling."

"You are one confident feller, aren't you?"

"I try not to feel deprived."

"If you can do what you did to me again, I'll believe anything you say."

"Hold on, dearie. We're about to take another ride."

He rammed her deep, then slid back slow across the sensitive tip of her clit-trigger. Halfway across, Alice screamed. Her back arched and she quivered all over like a skewered animal.

Doc smiled to himself.

Alice's eyes were closed.

She was in another world.

Raider couldn't stand it any longer.

That dangling leg got to him finally.

Lorelei watched him, amused, as he rose from his chair and stalked over to her.

He took her hand and pulled her to her feet. All the time they had been talking, he had been observing her mannerisms. There was something oddly familiar about her, yet he knew he had never seen her before. He would have remembered.

"You're not going to rape me, are you? I heard that Pinkertons were gentlemen."

Raider said nothing. Instead, he pulled her into his arms and kissed her hard on the mouth and he felt her body relax. He crushed her breasts against his chest, felt them mash and yield. He probed her mouth with his tongue until she began to answer him in kind. His hand slid down her back and grabbed a handful of buttock. He squeezed.

Lorelei gasped when he broke the kiss.

Her eyes danced with fire.

"You do rape a woman," she husked. "You rape with your eyes. With your mouth. With your tongue."

"Rape is something you do to a woman against her will."

"Yes."

"You invite a man to do things to you."

"Do something to me, Raider."

Her mouth opened invitingly. Her lips were wet. Her breasts rose and fell. He felt the heat of her loins. His cock began to swell and throb. He reached around her back and unfastened the buttons of her dress. He pressed his loins into hers and she began to undulate her hips, grinding into him, rubbing his swollen organ against the softness of her sex.

Her dress whispered to the floor. The cutaway brassiere was the next to go. He pulled her panties down and knelt at her feet. He burrowed his face into her muff and began tonguing the sex-cleft, gripping her bare buttocks with both hands.

Her legs quivered with a raging desire as his tongue slithered inside the moist flesh of her pussy. Her hands fell to his head. Fingers twined through his thick shock of hair. She pulled him into her loins until he smothered with the reek of her musk.

She shuddered as an orgasmic spasm rippled through her body.

"Hurry," she said. "Take your clothes off while I turn down the bed."

Raider stripped quickly, hearing the thud of her shoes as she kicked them off, the rustle of sheets as she made the bed ready for them.

He went to her, looking at her tall naked body afire from the lamp glow or the excitement in her veins. The thatch between her legs was dark, and he knew she had dyed her hair blond. She opened her arms in a beckoning gesture.

She was a tigress unleashed when he took her in a crushing embrace. Her mouth seemed to be everywhere. Her legs wrapped around him. They wallowed as they kissed passionately. She grabbed his cock with a desperate hand and twisted around so that she could take it into her mouth. She bobbed up and down on his stalk until it was slick with her saliva, until the veins threatened to burst.

She panted and gasped with the breathlessness of desire, and her hands turned to raking claws that scoured his flesh with the urgency of her passion. He pinned her down, pried her legs apart, and entered her even as she squirmed, out of control.

Lorelei was a savage wanton. Hungry. A woman in season. There seemed no end to her, no end to her energy. Raider sweated, and so did she, until their bodies were sleek in the rose light from the lamps, until the sheets were soggy and roiled into swirls of cloth.

She clawed and scratched every time an orgasm rippled through her flesh. She moaned and screamed softly when he slowed or speeded up. He took her from behind and let her ride him from on top. Her eyes glazed over and closed as she pumped him into her cunt, slid up and down his cock, skewering her pussy on the swollen mass until she quickened and fell on his chest, caught in the throes of a shattering climax.

"Now!" she screamed, when he was back atop her. "Come, come!"

Her fingers pulled at his arms as if to draw him deeper. Her hips moved in a swift, desperate rhythm, and Raider let himself go. He rode with her to the heights of her passion, and then his seed burst from his sac in a soundless explosion.

Fireworks and drumbeats. The long fall from a dizzying height. They crashed together, sated, stunned, bewildered. He sagged atop her sweat-sleek body, and she played with his hair, twirling it between her fingers.

"Who are you?" she asked. "Where did you come from?"

Raider was jolted back to reality.

"I am your enemy," he said.

"Not tonight. Not now. You are my lover. My rapist."

He propped himself up on one arm and looked at her.

Her eyes were shadowy with a fleeting sadness.

"Damn you, woman," he growled. "Why couldn't you be what you were meant to be?"

"But I am," she said, and the cloudiness went out of her eyes.

"No, you're not. You're a killer, and you—"

She put a finger over his lips.

"Don't," she said. "Don't say any more. You don't know who I am nor how I came to be here. Someday you might, but not now. And if you do find out, it will probably be too late for you. It's already too late."

He looked at her blonde hair and at the dark thatch between her legs.

He looked at her bone structure, and remembered certain expressions on her face when they made love.

She didn't have the permanent scowl, nor the ulcers. But she had something else eating at her. From inside. She had knifed Roger Welch in cold blood; she had driven a fist into Doc's face.

He knew who she was.

Goldberg had hinted at it, and Raider remembered that.

Lorelei Standish was Josiah Benedict Abernathy's daughter.

Doc dressed carefully. He felt good.

Alice Cummings watched him in fascination.

"Doc," she said from her perch on the bed. She was already dressed. She had bathed them both with washcloth and water and had dried Doc off with a towel before he did the same to her.

"Yes?"

"Most of the girls here want to get out."

"I gathered that."

"Can you help us?"

"How many of you are unhappy with this situation?"

"Me, Laura Lee Hope, and a girl named Nadine Orwell. She works here."

Raider had told him about Laura Lee.

"I can help you, if you help me," Doc said.

"I'll try."

"I'm looking for a short man. Probably keeps to himself. But he would be quiet, unobtrusive."

"He doesn't come here."

"No, probably not. But he would have something to do with making the Pecos dollars. He would be close to Big Jake."

Alice's expression brightened.

"There is such a man. But no one pays him much mind. He lives alone, in a small house at the end of Main Street. We hardly ever see him. But I've seen Big Jake go there, and Lorelei. He has a visitor staying with him now. A man who came to town a few weeks ago."

"Do you know the name of the short man?"

Doc finished buttoning his vest and drew on his coat.

"Albert something."

"Metz?"

"Yes, I think so."

Weatherbee's pulse quickened. He walked over to the bed.

"Now, think carefully," he said. "Can you describe the man who's staying with Metz?"

Alice thought about it. She squinted her eyes, trying to think.

"Tall man. Very businesslike. He has a sour expression on his face. He takes medicine. Drinks a lot of milk. We hear gossip all the time here. He has some kind of stomach trouble."

"My dear, you are precious beyond words."

"Does this help you?"

"It does, it does." Doc pecked her on the cheek and took

her hand. "Now, let's go downstairs and have a nightcap. I must be on my way."

"Doc," she said. "It was good. The best I ever had. I don't pay attention to most men. I don't really look at them. I just want to get it over with. You were different."

He patted the back of her hand.

"Now, now, let's not get carried away."

He walked toward the door and froze.

A board creaked outside.

Someone was out there. Had been. Listening.

Alice's hand squeezed his.

They both heard retreating footsteps.

Doc dashed to the door and unlocked it. He flung it open and stuck his head out to peer down the hall. He saw only a shadowy figure turning the corner.

"Damn," he muttered.

"Who was it?" she said.

"I don't know. A customer," he lied.

Alice breathed a sigh of relief.

Doc wondered how much Grabowski had heard. How long he had been standing outside the door.

"Alice, if you need me, I'm at the Silver Dollar."

"Why? Is something wrong?"

"I don't know," he said.

But something was wrong. If Grabowski had heard what Alice had told him, she could be in danger.

He thought of the man visiting Albert Metz.

Alice had described him well enough so that Doc had no doubt who was alive and well and living in Pecos Gulch.

Abernathy.

CHAPTER SIXTEEN

Big Jake Loman, neé Branfield Logan, was a striking figure of a man. He was big, big all over. Straight-backed as a military man. His chest was wide and square. He seemed to have no hips at all, his bulk tapering down to strong legs that held him straight when he walked or stood. Most impressive of all was his face, which was square-jawed, chiseled. His locks were long and flowing, with just a tinge of gray at the temples. He wore clothes that fit well—tailored jackets and perfectly tapered trousers. His was a commanding presence, and he exuded a magnetism that was startling. He had pale blue eyes that glinted with a hidden fervor, as if he were an evangelist continually in the throes of receiving revelations from on high. His lips were full and pouty, the lower one drooping onto a cleft chin.

When he walked into the saloon at the Silver Dollar, conversations sank into silence like stones into a deep lake. He towered over the men standing at the bar, and when he spoke, his voice boomed, full of resonance and power.

"Barkeep," he roared. "Drinks on the house. The rest of the night."

"Yes, sir, Big Jake," said the bartender with a grin. Men rushed to the bar, scarcely believing what they had heard.

Big Jake himself had the first drink, and he raised his glass of whiskey in a toast.

"I've brought my daughter to the Gulch," he said, "and there'll be prosperity for all."

A loud cheer rose in the saloon, and men who had heard the noise began drifting in from the lobby, from outside, and from the hotel rooms. Extra bartenders were pressed into service.

Big Jake took his drink and retreated to his favorite table in the rear. Men slapped him on the back and cheered him for being such a good fellow. A moment after he sat down, Jess Burnett made his way through the throng. He stopped near Loman's table.

"Sit down, Jess," said Loman, "and give me all the news."

"There's plenty," said Burnett, with a frown. "None of it too good."

"There's nothing we can't handle, is there now?"

"No, sir," he replied sheepishly.

"Then let's have it. Simple and straight."

Jess told him about the Pinkertons, about Laura Lee, and about the shooting of Two Fingers.

"Merle, he got hit. Not bad. In the leg. He's sore and limping around."

"The Pinkertons, they get to Al Metz yet?"

"No, sir. They're over to the Pleasure Palace. I think the one they call Doc was out to the mine."

A shadow seemed to pass over Loman's face.

"Well," he said, "we'll just give those boys some rope, let them hang themselves. Meantime, you see how Jenkins is. Tell him to limp over there to the Palace and keep an eye on those two jaspers. And here's what I want you to tell Ski. . . ."

He leaned over and whispered instructions into Burnett's ear. Jess left immediately to find Merle Jenkins.

Big Jake did not stay long after that. By that time the saloon was full to capacity. Loman smiled and waved to the men getting drunk on his money. He wanted them to get good and likkered up, for Pecos Gulch had served its purpose, and it was time to pull out.

He walked down the street to the house where Albert Metz was staying.

He knocked on the door.

Metz did not open it.

Abernathy did.

* * *

Doc waited in the parlor for Raider.

Most of the girls were busy. A man came in and said something to another that Doc couldn't hear.

The second man let out a whoop.

"Hey, Ski," he said to Grabowski. "Your boss is back in town, and he's buying free drinks at the Silver Dollar."

"He's early," said Grabowski, but a knowing look passed across his face. A moment later he threw down his towel and headed for the back hallway. Doc frowned. Something was up. He didn't like it.

A few seconds later, Raider rattled through the beaded curtains.

He was grinning.

Doc stood up.

"Wipe that grin off your face and let's get out of here. Fast."

"Hey, Doc, don't be so pushy. I'm just getting my second wind."

Doc jabbed Raider in the gut, hard.

"Now," he said, *sotto voce*. "There's something brewing, and we need to do some talking."

"Yeah, I know. Grabowski's back there with Lorelei now. Big Jake's back in town."

Doc could see that Raider was still in a fog. He shoved him toward the door. Raider tried to resist, but Doc was determined. Outside, he turned to square off against his partner.

"You idiot!" said Doc. "We don't have time for this. Loman's buying free drinks for the town at the Silver Dollar."

"Well, hell, what are we waiting for? Let's go meet the bastard and get some of his free booze."

"All right, Raider," said Doc, in exasperation. "But will you give me ten minutes of your time first? Ten minutes. We can compare notes, and if you still want to get soused, I'll go with you. Fair enough?"

"Fair enough."

The two men moved off into the shadows. There they had a view of the front porch of the Pleasure Palace, but they could not be seen. They hunkered down next to a small sand hill. Doc stuck a cheroot in his mouth but didn't light it. Before they had a chance to start talking, a man ran down the street and hit the steps in full stride.

"Jess Burnett," said Raider quickly.

"In a hurry."

The front door banged as Burnett went inside. The two men who had been talking about the free drinks left a moment later. Then Burnett came out, followed by Grabowski.

"What if they don't come back?" said the Pole.

"No matter. Big Jake's covering all bets. You just do what he said. Merle will be along in a minute. You know what to do."

"Jesus Christ, Jess, I had the bastards here not five minutes ago."

"They might come back, Ski."

Burnett left, and Grabowski stayed on the porch.

"The next man up will be Jenkins," said Doc. "We might find out something."

"I wonder what they've got planned for us, Doc."

"Can't you guess?"

Raider felt the hackles rise on the back of his neck. He could guess. As they waited, Lorelei came out on the porch. She spoke so low the operatives couldn't hear what she said.

"Here he comes now," said Grabowski.

A man limped out of the shadows and up to the porch.

"Them Pinkertons still in there?" asked Merle Jenkins.

"Hell no. Where in hell were you tonight?"

"One of them winged me. In the leg."

"Dumb bastard," said Grabowski.

Lorelei shoved Grabowski aside and moved out on the porch. She looked down at Jenkins.

"You stay here, Merle. Do your job. Ski will back you. I ought to fire you for the way you messed things up tonight."

"Miss Lorelei, you were there too. That feller shoots like a rattlesnake bites."

"I'm not interested in excuses. Ski, you know where to find me."

"Yes'm," said Grabowski.

Lorelei walked back to the door and reached inside. When she turned around, she had a medium-sized purse in her hand. It had a long strap, and she slung it over her shoulder. She walked down the steps and headed in the direction of Metz's house. Grabowski and Jenkins went back inside the whorehouse.

It was quiet.

"Do we follow her?" asked Doc.

"She's going to see her father," said Raider.

"Metz is her father?"

"Abernathy. And he's staying with Metz."

Doc took the cheroot from his mouth and let out a low whistle.

"How'd you find that out?"

Raider told him.

"Now we talk," said Doc. They got up, stretched, and moved a few yards farther away from Palace.

"Looks like things are coming to a head, Raider. Abernathy, who's supposed to be dead, is here, and Loman's back a day early. If he's buying drinks for the town, it's for a damned good reason. That man hasn't made any false moves, none that I know of, all the time we've been on his trail."

Raider nodded. He told Doc about the building he suspected of being a miniature mint, but wondered out loud why it was idle yet guarded.

"Could be that this whole thing is a sham," said Doc. "The town, the Pecos dollars."

Raider let the words sink in. He thought back to the time when he had first come on the case, to all the strange twists it had taken. There were the baron, Roger Welch, Goldberg, and radiating outward was the awesome presence of the

Denver mint. And its head, Abernathy. The fake murder of a man who resembled Abernathy was elaborate. It had almost worked.

"Doc," he said finally. "I think you've hit on it. Those Pecos dollars. There's a big robbery two years ago. Three men are murdered. Then, nothing. Two long years of silence. Not a trace of the bandits, not a track, not a clue."

"Then," continued Doc, excited, "all of a sudden those Pecos dollars start popping up all over the country. Right in the middle of the controversy about trade dollars."

"Why go to all the trouble of melting down perfectly good dollars and making counterfeits?"

"Do you know?" asked Doc.

"I'm beginning to get a bad feeling about those dollars. Like bait. Like something thrown out there to sucker us in here. Into a trap."

Doc waited a long time before he said anything.

"No, Raider, not bait. Something else. Something bigger. We just got caught in the web, like flies. You have to ask yourself why. Why?"

"I'm lost. None of it makes any sense. Here's Big Jake Loman. Hiding as a minister for years. Real name Logan. His daughter works at the mint. And Lorelei Standish, Abernathy's daughter. She worked at the mint too. All these people, and this counterfeit fucking town. Somebody's gone to a lot a trouble to pull the wool over our eyes, and it doesn't make any goddamned sense. A hundred thousand dollars, and all those good men, dead, and these bastards are turning out phony Pecos dollars that...hell, the government could just declare them worthless and that would put Loman and company out of business."

"Raider! You've got it!"

"Got what?"

"The answer. Don't you see it yet?"

"Hell no. I feel like tucking my tail between my legs and going into Santa Fe for a good long drunk. Let Wagner handle it. Let the Pinkerton brothers get someone else on this case. It's got me buffaloed."

"No it hasn't." Doc was excited. He talked fast and kept spitting out chunks of tobacco ground off the end of his cheroot."You said it. Abernathy. Everything revolves around him. His daughter, Loman's daughter, the fake homocide at the railway station. It was Abernathy all the time. Albert Metz. They both used to work together at the Philadelphia mint. It must have started there. At least the original idea, the scheme. And, oh what a beautiful scheme it was."

"Doc, are you sober?"

"Sober and sane as a judge. Come on, Raider, there's a lot to do. I'm going to Santa Fe to send a message to Wagner. I'm supposed to meet Spooner tonight and find out about those samples. I think we're just about to wrap up this case."

"Look, Doc, you still haven't told me what I'm supposed to have figured out."

"No time now. Besides, I'm not dead sure. I ought to know by morning. Can you handle things with Spooner? If he says there's no silver at that mine, then get him out of town fast. No reason for him to get caught in the crossfire. If it does assay out, we'll need him when we go in there."

"In where?"

"The mine."

"You think there's silver there?"

"Not in a million years, Raider."

CHAPTER SEVENTEEN

The two men split up. Doc hurried off up the street, staying in the shadows. Raider gave him a good lead, then walked to the hotel where Doc had told him Winton Spooner was staying.

The Pecos Hotel was virtually deserted. Down the street, the Silver Dollar saloon was crammed with townspeople taking advantage of Big Jake's generosity. Raider didn't bother trying to find out which room the geologist was in. Instead, he yelled out his name.

"Spooner!"

No answer. Raider yelled again, walking up and down the hallway.

An old man, evidently partially deaf, stuck his head out of a door.

"Eh?" he asked.

"Looking for a man named Spooner. Know what room he's in?"

"Spooner?"

"He works with rocks."

"Oh, thet one. Heard him pounding rocks with a hammer. Down the hall there. Number ten."

Raider knocked on the door labeled #10.

The door swung open.

Tiny cat claws prickled Raider's skin.

The furniture in the room was in disarray. Raider saw a pair of boots jutting out from under an overturned table. His stomach squirmed with a sudden uneasiness.

"Spooner?"

He walked over to the boots and lifted the table.

The geologist lay face down, sprawled in a pool of blood.

Raider knelt down and put a finger to the carotoid artery in Spooner's neck. There was no pulse. He touched the blood. It was still faintly warm. He turned Spooner over and felt the bile rise up in his throat.

"Christ!" he muttered.

Someone had shoved a knife in Spooner's gut, rammed it up under his rib cage, and twisted it. Raider looked at the wound closely. There were two wounds visible when he wiped the blood away with the tail of Spooner's shirt. The first wound had been caused by the knife going straight in. Such a knife thrust would double a man over. The next and final thrust had been delivered while Spooner was bent over. The blade had gone up under the ribs to the heart. A quick twist and the arteries had been severed, judging from the amount of blood on the floor.

Spooner had evidently bled to death quite soon after that last plunge of the blade.

Raider fought the sickness down as he stood up, giddy.

"Ten minutes," he said to himself. "No more than fifteen. Ten lousy minutes."

He looked around the room. Papers were scattered everywhere. They left a trail, as if someone had gathered them up and dropped them. One window was wide open, the shade pulled up. Crumpled papers lay under the sill. Raider leaned outside and looked down. There were more papers outside.

Someone had come in, he reasoned, and shoved a knife in Spooner's gut. He had doubled over in pain and staggered backwards. The follow-up had been the lethal stab with the knife. Spooner had crashed against the table and overturned it on top of him. It had not taken long for him to die.

Raider picked up some of the papers and looked at them. They were full of figures and notes he couldn't decipher. Another check of the room revealed the tools of Spooner's trade: scales, crucibles, Bunsen burners, a hammer, tongs. The room smelled of blood and smoke. Crushed stone lay on top of a low dresser, next to a Bunsen burner and scales.

A patch of white caught Raider's eyes. He stooped down

and pulled a piece of foolscap from under the dresser.

This paper too was scrawled with figures and notes.

He studied it for several moments.

Spooner had written down the results of tests he had made on several samples of ore.

At the bottom, in block letters, he had inscribed the conclusion he had reached.

NO TRACES OF SILVER IN ANY OF THE SAMPLES.

Raider folded the paper carefully and tucked it into his pocket.

He left the room and walked back down the hall. He knocked on the door where he had seen the old man.

"You see anyone go into that room a while ago?" he asked the man.

"That stranger's room? Yep. Saw a woman, tall she was. Knocked on his door. Went right in."

"See her come back out?"

"No, sir. Far as I know, she didn't. You come along, yellin' and hollerin'."

"Know who she was?"

The old man cocked his eye and looked at Raider slyly.

"Sure I do."

"Who was she?"

"You don't know? Hell, you was just there."

"She's gone."

"Ah, I heard something out back. Thought it was a cat. No, no cats here. A dog maybe. Made a racket."

Raider's patience was wearing thin.

"The woman. Who was she?"

"Oh, her. Yep, seed her around. Tall woman. Purty as a snake. Wondered why she come to this hotel. Thought it must be she took a fancy to the young stranger. He made a lot of racket too. Pounding on something. Sounded like rocks. Young for a miner. Must have found some ore. Thought about it a lot. I keep track of everybody. Don't know where everyone went tonight. Place cleared out like they was—"

"Look, old man, I don't mean to be impolite, but this is

important. If you know who that tall woman was, tell me."

"Why, it was the Lorelei. That's what I call her. The Lorelei. Purtiest woman in town, but a heart as dark as Hades. Sinful woman, she is."

"Yes," said Raider tightly. "Thanks."

"Say, feller, who you be?"

Raider didn't answer.

He turned on his heel and was gone before the old-timer realized it.

"Strange goings-on," the old man muttered. "Strange."

Raider's stomach boiled with acrid juices. He wanted a drink. He wanted to keep running and never look back. He had made a mistake. He had misjudged Lorelei Standish.

He had thought she was going to Metz's house, to see her father.

Maybe to see Big Jake.

Instead she had gone to the Pecos Hotel and knifed Winton Spooner to death.

Where was she now?

One of several places.

She'd have blood on her hands.

The Pleasure Palace.

He headed there, back to the place where he had lain with her not an hour before. How could a woman with a body like that, with a talent like that, kill in cold blood? He didn't know, but his stomach twisted into agonized knots. He wanted to blow her to hell, and at the same time he thought of her beauty and the way she made love. A waste of good woman.

He had no authority to arrest her, but he knew that if she wasn't put in irons she would kill again.

By all that was right, he ought to ride to Santa Fe and bring in the territorial marshal.

He kept seeing Spooner's face in death, the knife wounds.

The first one had looked familiar. The same as the one he'd seen in Roger Welch.

Lorelei.

He hoped she was at the Pleasure Palace, and the minute he thought that, his stomach roiled with a sudden spasm. At the same time, he hoped she would not be there. He wanted to put his hands around her throat and choke her senseless. He wanted to make her scream for mercy. He wanted, maybe, to make her tell him why she had killed and why she herself deserved to live.

If she did deserve to live.

The Pleasure Palace looked different when he returned. It took him a moment to realize that there was only a single lamp burning.

Yet the door was open.

Raider stepped onto the porch and stood to one side of the door.

"Anybody there?" he called.

"We're closed. Everybody's gone to the Silver Dollar."

"I want to see Lorelei."

"Who's that?"

"Raider."

He heard footsteps, a tinkle of glass. Someone struck a match. Another lamp began to glow.

"She's not here," said Grabowski, coming to the door.

"Where is she?"

"I don't know. We're closed for the night."

Raider pushed open the door and stepped inside. He heard footsteps in the back. On the stairs.

"I think she is here," he said.

Grabowski stood in shadow, next to the bar. Both hands were visible. But the stairs creaked, and Raider tried to peer past the beaded curtains. He saw only more shadows.

The stairs creaked again.

Raider heard a loud *click*.

He went into a crouch, at the same moment pulling his pistol.

As he cleared leather, a pistol boomed beyond the curtains. Smoke and flame belched from an unseen gun. Raider fired in that same split second, aiming just below the flash of orange flame. A lead projectile whistled past his ear. Close.

He heard the curtains rattle, saw beads burst and shatter. The curtains swayed and a man grunted in pain.

Merle Jenkins coughed and staggered through the curtains. A red stain spread over his belly. His pistol hung loose in his dangling hand. His face contorted in pain, drained of color.

"Bastard," he croaked.

He pitched forward and fell face down, hitting the floor with a shattering thud.

Out of the corner of his eye, Raider saw Grabowski move. At first he was only a blurred shadow, then his bulk loomed up on him. The Pole held something in his hand. Raider tried to turn and bring his pistol to bear. But Grabowski was too fast. He swung his arm, and Raider tried to duck.

Something solid, wooden, smashed into his forehead.

He tried to stay conscious. He fought against the darkness welling up in his mind. Dazzling lights danced in his skull. He threw up an arm as he saw the club come down again. He heard a terrible crunch, felt a sticky wetness where the blow had struck.

The Pinkerton felt his knees buckle. Pain throbbed through his brain.

Then the darkness washed over him as he crumpled to the floor.

A few seconds later Lorelei stepped through the beaded curtains. She had changed into dark trousers and shirt and tied her hair up in a bun. She held a towel in her hands and was scrubbing her hands dry.

She looked at Jenkins on the floor. A pool of blood spread from underneath him. Raider lay sprawled on his side, his hat bashed in, his head bloody. Grabowski stood over him with the bloodstained club.

"Is Merle dead?"

Grabowski nodded. "Do you want me to finish off the Pinkerton?" he asked.

Lorelei's eyes slitted.

She looked at Raider's helpless form. She balled up the towel in her hands and threw it on the floor.

"His partner left town, but he'll be back. We may need this one alive for a while longer. Take him over to Al's."

"That where you're going?"

"Yes. You'll be needed there. Bring the wagon."

"What's Big Jake going to do?" he asked.

"We're leaving. I think he's going to burn the town down."

"That why he's getting everyone drunked up?"

"That's why, Ski."

"A lot of people are going to be fried."

"Yes. The tragedy will give us all just that much more time."

"Pretty smart."

"Big Jake knows what he's doing."

She went to a closet off the parlor, took out a felt hat, and put it on. From a distance she looked like a man. A tall man. She strapped on a pistol. Under her belt, tucked inside her trousers, the haft of a deadly bowie knife jutted up over the waistband.

Despite himself, Grabowski shuddered.

Raider was only semiconscious; he heard what they had said, but he could make no sense of it. The syllables were like cotton balls soaked in water. They bobbed up and down in his consciousness. Some part of him grabbed at them and tried to put them together.

All he knew was that something terrible was going to happen, and he was helpless to do anything about it.

"See you at Al's," said Lorelei, stepping through the front door. "Better tie Raider up good before you load him in the wagon."

"What about Merle?"

"Leave him. He's not going anywhere."

Grabowski swallowed hard.

Sometimes he wondered if he was not in way over his head.

CHAPTER EIGHTEEN

Doc Weatherbee climbed down from the pole, panting from the exertion.

Despite Judith's shying at every shadow along the rutted road from Pecos Gulch, he had made good time, reaching the outskirts of Santa Fe in just under four hours. Now, the scent of pine-studded hills wafted down to him on the flat. He set up the gravity battery and the key and worked by faint lantern light. He had shinnied up the first telegraph pole he had found and hoped he could get through to Wagner in Chicago.

He tapped the key, sending Morse code at close to thirty words a minute.

The message, carefully composed on the long wagon ride, hummed along the wires.

REQUEST IMMEDIATE AUDIT DENVER MINT STOP ABERNATHY ALIVE PECOS GULCH STOP SUGGEST STOLEN SILVER RUSE STOP POSSIBLE COVER-UP FOR BIGGER THEFT STOP URGENT WEATHERBEE.

The wait for Wagner's reply seemed interminable. Doc lit a cheroot and shivered in the night chill.

Finally, the answering key began to clatter.

AUDIT COMPLETED TEN DAYS AGO STOP U.S. MARSHALS EN ROUTE PECOS GULCH WITH WARRANTS FOR ABERNATHY'S ARREST STOP DETAIN IF NECESSARY STOP OTHER WARRANTS INCLUDED STOP ABERNATHY EMBEZZLED ONE MILLION GOLD STOP AUTHORIZE USE OF FORCE TO HOLD PRISONERS FOR U.S. MARSHALS WALES AND GOODE STOP WAGNER.

Weatherbee acknowledged the message. His heart pounded, and his finger shook on the key.

Wagner did not tap back.

Doc scrambled back up the pole, his fingers cold. A quarter hour later he had turned the wagon back toward Pecos Gulch. It would be dawn before he could arrive, even if Judith hurried. A cool wind blew down out of the mountains, and the mule stepped out with no urging on his part.

The enormity of Wagner's message slowly sank in, and the shaking in his hands subsided.

So he was right. The robbery was only a cover-up for an embezzlement. Slick. Abernathy was guilty as sin. But was there somebody behind him? Or had he figured it out for himself and recruited the others with the promise of a larger reward.

Now it all made sense.

Or most of it.

He knew now why Abernathy was in town and why Big Jake had offered free liquor at the Silver Dollar saloon.

They were going to pull out and abandon the town. Perhaps tonight or early in the morning. What better way to assure that no questions would be asked than to get most of the town's denizens drunk.

Suddenly another thought occurred to him.

If they were pulling out, then Raider's life wasn't worth a tinker's damn.

And neither was his.

Raider lay crunched in a corner of the house, his hands tied behind his back. He kept his eyes closed and listened to the conversation, the noise of people coming and going. Outside he heard horses and the creak of wagons, the slap of leather traces.

The outlaws were loading goods into the wagons.

What? Stolen silver?

He heard Lorelei's voice and could identify Abernathy's. One voice stood out above the others, and he guessed it belonged to Big Jake. Sometimes the voices would come into the room, and he knew they were looking at him. There was always someone with him. He could hear him breathing, but he never spoke.

Finally he found out who was guarding him.

"He still out, Jess?" boomed the voice of Loman.

"Hasn't moved," said Burnett.

"Ski, you really coldcocked him," said Big Jake.

"He might not never wake up," said Grabowski.

"Lorelei," said Loman. "You still think it wise to let him live?"

"His partner, Weatherbee, is still missing. I don't know if he left town or is just hiding out. I thought we'd use Raider as bait in case he shows up."

"I want to be all packed up by first light. Ski, you got those torches fixed up."

"Yeah. About an hour before we leave, Jess and I will spread coal oil all over town. It ought to go up fast. Wind came up an hour ago."

"Good."

The voices faded away, and Raider listened to Burnett breathing. The fuzziness had receded, and he realized that what he had heard just now matched what Lorelei had said to Grabowski earlier. They were planning to burn down the town when they left. Hundreds of innocent people were in danger. And he was powerless to warn them.

Raider tried to work his hands free of the rope bonds. Grabowski's knots were tight.

He nodded in and out of consciousness. Later, he slept. When he awoke it was quiet, except for the sound of Burnett's snoring. There were no voices. He opened one eye and looked around the room. It was bare except for a table and chairs. Burnett had his feet propped up on one and lay with his head back on another. The lamp burned low.

A sound froze him.

He closed his eye, then reopened it to a tiny slit.

Someone tiptoed toward the room.

Burnett moved but did not awaken.

Raider waited, wondering who might be in the house. Someone who, like him, didn't belong there.

* * *

Janet Logan crept quietly into the room.

She carried a knife and Raider's pistol.

His eyes opened wide in surprise.

She saw him look at her and she put a finger to his lips. She bent over him and reached behind him with the knife. She cut the bonds fastening his wrists together. He took the knife from her and cut his leg bonds. He stood up gingerly, suddenly dizzy. She handed him the pistol.

He walked over to Burnett.

"What are you going to do?" she whispered.

Raider raised his pistol, holding it by the barrel. His hand arced downward. The butt struck Burnett behind the ear. He slid to the floor without regaining consciousness.

Janet shuddered.

"Thanks for cutting me loose," he said. "Where are they?"

"At the workshop. Where they mint the Pecos dollars."

"You're not one of them?"

She shook her head.

"Why'd you come here?"

"They were going to kill you. Doc, too. Where is he?"

"Gone. What about you. Does your father know you're here?"

"He . . . he thinks I'm with Laura Lee. She's frightened. We all are."

"All?"

"Laura Lee, me, Nadine Orwell, Alice Cummings. We ran off and hid in one of the buildings they've cleaned out. I saw Ski bring you here. I heard Lorelei say she was going to kill you."

"What about your father?"

"Big Jake? He . . . he's not my father. He killed my father and took his place, his name."

"What?"

"I haven't seen my father since I was a little girl. But Big Jake's not him. He said he was, and I believed him until I saw what he was. We can't stay here, though. They'll be back at any time. They're taking everything and going to Mexico, then to South America."

"Are you sure Big Jake's not your father?"

"I wasn't until this morning, before we left Santa Fe. He...he came into my room and took off his clothes. My father had a large birthmark on his stomach. This man had no such mark. He...he tried to rape me. I screamed, and he shut me up. I asked him what he did to my father, and he said I wouldn't have to worry about it. He...he bragged about it, Raider. He murdered my father a little over two years ago and assumed his identity. He knew his habits, imitated his handwriting, everything."

"But surely he would have been found out. Your father was a well-known minister."

"Was. Big Jake said he was in a kind of sanitarium. He was a victim of John Barleycorn, I'm afraid. As I said, I haven't seen my father since I was a little girl. Then this man started to write to me, said he wanted to make a home for me."

"You weren't in on the robbery, then?"

"No! You must believe me. I knew nothing about it, but I found out something else. I—"

Suddenly, Janet Logan's eyes opened wide and she stared at the doorway.

A small, wiry man in his fifties stood there, the deadly snouts of a double-barreled shotgun pointed at her and Raider.

"You found out too much, I'm afraid," said the man.

Raider knew who he was. The accent was thick, gutteral. German. The man wore glasses that magnified his cobalt eyes. He wore a dark pin-striped suit. He was under five feet tall, with thick lips and hawkish features. He had seen him only once before, in the dark, but he would not forget him.

"Albert Metz, isn't it?" said Raider.

Metz smiled thinly.

"We have met before."

"Almost," said Raider.

He noticed that the shotgun was not cocked. That gave him a slight edge. But Metz had come up on them like a cat. He was fast, as Raider knew. And deadly. His face betrayed no expression as he sized up his chances. A blast from the shotgun at that range would tear them both in half. Could he risk Janet's life to save his own? How many seconds would it take him to clear leather, hammer back, and fire? Metz's left hand held the sawed-off shotgun. His right hovered like a bird above the twin hammers.

It would be close.

Mighty damned close.

A man's lifetime could go by pretty quick under such circumstances. Raider found himself wondering about Doc, what he would do in such a situation. He thought about Janet Logan, caught up in a situation she barely understood, and a whole bunch of people in a town that was about to be burned to the ground. He thought about Mary Brown back in Denver, whose husband Leonard had been gunned down in the sweet prime of his life by a bunch of greedy cutthroats. He thought of the girls in Pecos Gulch caught up in white slavery against their will. He thought about Big Jake, who had killed a helpless man and taken over his identity for base and illegal reasons. He thought about Lorelei and her blood-soaked knife. He thought of Abernathy and Albert Metz, a quiet man who had a killer's heart and an artist's hands. What made people tick? What made them good? What made them go sour? What made them go so bad they spoiled life for everyone else?

The thoughts took but a fraction of a second or two.

Raider made his decision.

There were only two roads, really.

One led to life, the other to death.

Ultimately, it was the same road.

And a gambler banks on odds and the fatal turn of cards sometimes.

A man against the wall has no place to go.

Raider looked into the twin barrels of death, and he had his own life within reach: a Remington .44 in its hard leather holster—cold and unfeeling until cocked and triggered. Life within death.

He had the drunken town with its sotted inhabitants on his conscience.

And there was Doc Weatherbee and the code of the Pinkertons.

Albert Metz had pumped the deadly lead shot into Leonard Brown's body. Two years ago. A long time ago.

Raider's eyes turned cold like the dying coals in ashes. Banked fires of hatred that bored into Metz's eyes.

Everything boiled down to simple arithmetic. Law and order. Right and wrong. Life and death. Quick and slow.

Eternity balanced on the tip of a man's mind, like a straw caught on barbed wire when the wind is unsettled and circling. A roll of the dice, a turn of the cards.

One man could die. Or another. Both could die in a moment of squeezed triggers.

Raider narrowed it down as a man will whittle a pencil to a fine point. This could be his last moment of his life or Metz's. He could shave time only so fine, and then it would break. He had whittled it down this far. This was the edge—when time hung as still as an autumn leaf just barely attached to a limb. When death had not yet begun to rattle in the throat.

This was the time when a man made his move or died in his tracks.

Metz sensed the change in Raider.

His tongue flicked over dry lips.

His eyes batted.

Raider saw the signals and made his choice.

His right hand flashed toward his holster.

Janet Logan gasped and tried to scream.

Raider's pistol swung up in his hand, his thumb working, clawing.

Albert Metz banged his palm on the two hammers of the sawed-off shotgun. His movement was smooth, practiced.

The silence filled with the metallic *clack* of cocking mechanisms.

Raider moved and knocked Janet Logan down as his finger sought the trigger of his big-bore Remington.

Metz was fast. His finger wrapped around both triggers and pulled hard. His eyes flickered with a cold hatred.

The roar of weapons wiped out all thought, blanked out vision with red-orange flame and the quick hiss of leaden death. Smoke filled the air in acrid, suffocating clouds that blotted out the shooters and turned them into shadows.

A man cried out in pain.

A man fell, tumbling through thick white smoke.

A man died.

CHAPTER NINETEEN

Raider squeezed the trigger and dove sideways toward Janet. He landed atop her, covering her body from the shotgun's terrible twin blasts.

A rush of hot air blew at him as if someone had opened the door of a furnace.

Lethal lead pellets crashed into the window pane and spattered into the wall with a deadly rattle. Smoke and flame filled the room.

He twisted and cocked his pistol.

Acrid smoke scorched his lungs as he leveled the pistol at the doorway. A breeze drifted in through the shattered window, clearing the room of smoke. Raider's eyes watered as he tried to see if his bullet had drawn blood.

The dark form of Albert Metz appeared through the swirling fog of white smoke. The small man stood there, weaving slightly from side to side.

Slowly the scattergun slipped from the engraver's grasp. It clattered on the floor. Metz took a step forward and his legs went out from under him, collapsing like crutches made of rubber. He made a gurgling sound in his throat. Blood bubbled out of the corners of his mouth.

Raider stood up and walked toward the dying man.

He turned Metz over with a nudge of his boot.

The bullet had gone in just under the heart, into Metz's left lung. Blood pumped through the .44-caliber hole, dark against the black of the man's suit. In his back there was a hole the size of a man's fist. Janet stood up on wobbly legs, walked over to the Pinkerton, and held onto him for support. Raider eased the hammer down on his pistol and shoved it back in its holster. He rubbed his wrists where the rope had dug in.

"Is he . . . ?"

"Almost," said Raider to Janet.

"He used to be—"

"—one of the best engravers in the business. He's wolf meat now."

Metz blinked his eyes and opened his mouth to say something. Trickles of blood seeped out of both sides of his mouth. He sounded as if he was gargling.

"Was it worth it, Metz? How much silver did you get?"

"Gold," he hissed, his eyes blazing hatred. "A million in gold."

Raider looked at Janet.

"Gold?"

Janet shrugged.

"Gold," rasped Metz again. Then his eyes frosted over, dulled, as a death spasm rippled through his body. He made a gurgling sound in his throat. Blood bubbled up over his lips, onto his chin. Janet turned away, covering her eyes.

Metz's sphincter muscle loosened, filling the room with a stench.

Burnett moaned and came to. He shook his head; his hand started for his pistol.

"Don't do it, Burnett," said Raider.

"I can beat you."

"One question first." Burnett's hand held steady scant inches from the butt of his pistol. "Are you the one with the limp?"

Burnett's face told Raider that he had struck bone.

"You'll never know, bastard."

Burnett went for it. Raider was ready. Janet screamed, her senses glutted on sudden death.

The thin gunman was fast. Very fast.

Raider beat him by a millisecond. His pistol boomed and bucked in his hand. Burnett's face disappeared in a cloud of smoke and flame at close range. His pistol discharged, the lead streaking into the floor. The back of his head came apart in a rosy explosion of blood and shattered bone, spraying the wall with chunks of brain matter that slid slowly down after the smoke cleared.

Burnett collapsed in a dead heap.

Janet began to weep from fear.

"Steady," said Raider, touching her shoulder. He worked the ejector rod on his pistol, expelling empty brass hulls. He crammed two fresh bullets in the chambers, spun the cylinder, eased the hammer down from half-cock. He holstered his weapon and knelt over the dead gunman.

He jerked off Burnett's boots and pulled both trouser legs up. He winced as he saw the scars on one leg, the deep, twisted marks of old wounds. The leg had been broken at least twice, maybe three times. The bones had set crooked. Satisfied, Raider stood up and took Janet's hand.

"Come on," he said. "Let's get out of here. Where are the girls?"

"Hiding in the livery. They want me to see if I can bring them a wagon."

"Bad place. That place will go up like tinder. We'll get you all on horses, mine included, and then you give me an hour. Meet me at the Pleasure Palace. It's the safest place to be."

"But they said they can't go back there."

"They can go back there."

"I...I can't stand the killing anymore," she said numbly.

"There will be more," he said grimly.

An hour later, Raider stood against the side of the Pleasure Palace, his ear pressed against the wood.

His nostrils were filled with the cloying smell of coal oil. The town was soaked with it. The horses had been jittery, but he had gotten them saddled and had given instructions to the women.

The Silver Dollar was still in full swing, and he knew it must be at least three o'clock in the morning, maybe later.

Wagons were being loaded at the miniature mint, the

noises faint on the breeze that wafted his way.

He heard voices from inside the whorehouse.

The words were unintelligible, but he recognized the speakers. Grabowski and a man named Bill Anders.

Raider went to the back and found the rear door.

He went inside quietly, picking every step, testing each board before putting his full weight on it. He headed toward the faint light seeping down the hall from the front parlor.

He came to the foot of stairs without making any sound. Now he could understand the words Grabowski and Anders were saying.

Raider moved toward the beaded curtains.

"You get all of Miss Lorelei's things packed?" asked Grabowski.

"Everything, Ski. Must be a ton of clothes."

"They'll be by about dawn to load them up. Last stop before Mexico."

Anders laughed.

"It'll take the marshals months to figure this one out."

"We got two Pinkertons to take care of first."

"One down. One to go."

Raider's jaw set hard. A muscle quivered along the ridge of the bone.

The beaded curtain was a problem. He tried to picture in his mind where each man was sitting. The light was dim in the parlor. That was in his favor. As nearly as he could figure it, Anders was sitting by a window near the front door. To the right of it. Grabowski was probably on the divan, where he could watch the door.

"Somebody's coming," said Anders.

Raider leaned out and saw Anders by the window, peering through the curtains. His heart sank. He hoped it wasn't Janet and the other women.

"Make him out?" asked Grabowski.

"Yeah. It's Ned Pratt, and he's runnin' like his pants is afire."

"Pratt's supposed to be loading that minting equipment."

"Right now he's stompin' dirt, comin' lickety-split."

Raider braced himself. He didn't know who Pratt was, but time was running out. There was nothing to do but step into it when the time was right. In a way, the new man in the picture might be a help. He was a distraction. But he too would have to be taken care of if lives were to be saved.

Raider stood a foot back, in shadow, watching the front door. Anders got up and opened it as he heard footfalls on the front porch. Grabowski lit another lamp, apparently, because more light suddenly filled the room.

The man they called Pratt came through the door.

Raider recognized him: the man who had been braiding the rope outside the big building used for minting the Pecos dollars.

"What's the all-fired rush, Ned?" asked Anders.

"That mother-raping Pinkerton, that's what. He done got loose."

"Hey, he was tied up good," exclaimed Grabowski, stepping into Raider's view. The Pole held a lighted lamp in his hand.

"He had help, I reckon, but that ain't the bad part, Ski. He took out Burnett and Al Metz."

"Metz?" chorused Grabowski and Anders.

"Dead as doornails."

Raider stepped through the curtains sideways and cocked his pistol so they all would hear it. He leveled the barrel at Pratt's gut.

Grabowski and Anders turned their heads. Ned Pratt's eyes bulged in surprise.

"Don't anybody move," said the Pinkerton. "And do what I say. One at a time. Anders, you first. Drop your gunbelt."

Anders reached for his buckle with both hands.

Grabowski's face contorted as he was gripped with a blind rage.

He turned and hurled the lighted oil lamp straight at Raider.

Pratt's hand flew toward his pistol. Anders did the same.

Raider's pistol roared.

He ducked and threw up his left arm. The lamp struck it. The chimney broke on his elbow. He winced in pain. The lamp crashed to the floor and rolled in a semicircle. Flaming oil scattered in all directions.

Pratt doubled over as Raider's bullet ripped through his abdomen, smashing intestines to pulp before flattening against a hip bone with paralyzing force.

Anders cleared leather and started to turn for a shot at Raider.

Raider swung his pistol and thumbed the hammer back in one smooth, flowing motion.

Anders saw that he was going to be too late.

"No!" he yelled.

Raider shot him in the heart as flames licked the floor and rose up around his boots.

Grabowski ran right over Pratt, out the front door.

Anders went down at Raider's feet. A tongue of fire lapped at his hair.

Pratt collapsed, a dazed look on his face. His fingers relaxed and his pistol slipped out of his hand. A wall of flames, fed by the wood flooring, rose up. Raider could no longer see or hear Grabowski.

Furniture caught fire. Dry wood crackled and popped as the flames spread out of control.

Raider backed up, unable to go around through the front door.

He raced toward the back door.

Behind him, he heard Ned Pratt scream. He kept screaming as Raider leaped from the porch and ran around the building. Grabowski had disappeared.

His first priority was to find Janet and the other women and find them a place to hide out until he was finished with his business. Now that the Pleasure Palace was on fire, they would have to find a place just as safe. Safer. He stopped and shaded his face from heat. Flames leaped high in the air.

And then the whorehouse roared as the fire spread, blown

to a torch by the predawn breeze.

Ned Pratt stopped screaming.

Big Jake Loman angrily shoved cartridges into the chamber of the Winchester '73.

"I want that son of a bitch personally," he said to Grabowski.

"Shit, Jake, he took out Albert."

"Tricked him, likely. Or had help. Anybody seen that other Pinkerton—Weatherbee?"

Abernathy shook his head. His hands were trembling

Lorelei looked at the sky turning orange above the Pleasure Palace. Her face was frozen into a mask of hatred. All her clothes, all of her personal possessions were going up in smoke.

"He was alone," she said to Loman. "But somebody helped him get free."

"You know that?"

"I know it. That little bitch you brought here, Janet."

"We haven't got time for that," said Loman. "If we don't put this Raider down, he'll pick us off one at a time."

"You do what you want to do," she said. "But it's already turning light, and we've still got to get the loot from the phony mine."

"Yes," said Abernathy.

Loman rammed the last cartridge in the chamber and slammed the butt of the rifle down on the back of the wagon. The equipment was loaded on four wagons.

He looked at the eastern sky and saw the pale cream rent in the fabric of night. The light was spreading slowly across the horizon.

"You're right, Lorelei. Actually, our timetable is still pretty close to what we planned. Ski, you can start lighting those torches. Burn the Silver Dollar down first. I'll hunt the Pinkerton. Josiah, you and Lorelei take the last wagon down to the mine. Ski and I will join you as soon as we can. Fair enough?"

Abernathy nodded somberly.

Lorelei smiled.

"Don't let him die easy, Big Jake," she said. "Make it slow and hard."

CHAPTER TWENTY

Doc rolled into Pecos Gulch as the eastern horizon turned peach, then flame-orange. At the far end of Main Street, the Pleasure Palace, burning out of control, added to the luster of the morning sky.

Judith balked as the aroma of woodsmoke assailed her nostrils.

Raider ran toward him, waving both arms to stop him from proceeding further.

"Turn your wagon in, Doc," he shouted. "And come armed."

"What's going on?"

Raider, slightly out of breath, told him.

"We've got to get those people out of the Silver Dollar first," he said.

"Right," said Doc. He moved the wagon off on a side street and set the brakes. He and Raider ran down to the Silver Dollar. Drunks lay outside, passed out. One man sat on the porch watching the flames from the burning whorehouse lick the sky. He was too inebriated to comprehend what was happening.

The two Pinkertons rushed through the lobby of the hotel and into the saloon, pistols drawn.

The saloon was packed with die-hard drinkers. Men slept at tables and on the floor.

Raider and Doc fired their pistols into the air.

Heads turned.

"You've got about two seconds to get out," yelled Raider. "Big Jake's torching the town."

"Move!" said Doc. "Wake up the drunks, drag them outside."

"Bullshit!" yelled someone. "Big Jake wouldn't do that. Hell, he bought us all free drinks."

"Well, now you know why," said Raider sarcastically. "If you don't want to fry like grasshoppers in a Kansas wheatfield, you'll haul your asses out of here."

"He's lying!" slobbered another man.

"No, wait. I smell smoke!"

"Don't panic!" yelled Doc as men started to bolt for the door.

Raider started kicking chairs out from under sleeping men. A few men who were still standing started to jostle their companions to consciousness. The bartender leaped over the bar, his face white and drawn.

"Get 'em all out!" yelled Raider.

Sheepishly the bartender stopped his headlong race to freedom, picked up a drunk and began to lug him toward the hotel lobby.

"See if anybody's upstairs, Doc," said Raider. "I'll handle it down here."

A shadowy form passed by a window.

Grabowski held a torch in his hand.

Raider fired a shot through the window, shattering glass.

"Hurry up!" he hollered. "Ski's setting fire to the building now!"

Doc ran to the lobby. He took the stairs four at a time. He shouted, roused sleeping men. In Raider's room he threw his partner's stuff through the window. The room started to fill with smoke. Men got up from sleep; they babbled in the hallways. Smoke started to seep through the baseboards in the walls as Doc went to his own room and threw out his duds, hoping they would clear the building.

There wasn't enough water in the town to form a bucket brigade.

Doc checked as many rooms as he could and finally ducked though a swirl of smoke and clambered down the stairs behind two men carrying a third who had been overcome by smoke.

Raider met Doc in the lobby.

"All out, Doc?"

"Far as I know. What next?"

"Get Grabowski before he does any more damage. With this breeze, the whole damned town could go."

"You?"

"I'll get them started with shovels. They can throw dirt on the fire, dig some trenches. Then I'm going after Big Jake."

"Two marshals are coming. Abernathy made off with about a million in gold."

"I gathered that from Metz."

"Be careful, Raider."

"You worried about me, Doc?"

"See you."

Doc's face was smudged from soot. Raider laughed and shoved him out the door.

"Oh, Doc," he said. "If you get Grabowski, there are some women holed up who might need your attention."

"Who? Where?"

"Janet Logan, Laura Lee, Alice. One other."

"Safe now?"

"Don't know. I put them in Spooner's room. He checked out. I figured no one would go back there. I hauled him out back."

"Who killed Spooner?"

"Lorelei. With a knife. Same as Welch."

The heat from the saloon drove Doc back. He started to say something, but Raider was running down the street toward a blue roan tied to a hitch rail. Horses screamed in terror. Doc's gaze shifted to the Pecos Hotel, where Spooner had been. Men ran back and forth, shouting, disorganized. Doc looked at the Silver Dollar. The flames were all on the sides and back, held in check by the wind blowing north. If the breeze shifted, however, the whole street would go up like tinder.

Quickly he began to give orders as he ejected his spent hull and shoved another .38 into the empty cylinder. Two buildings away, a man ran from cover. Behind him, flames licked at the false front.

Grabowski!

Doc started after him. His pearl-gray derby blew off his head as the wind shifted from north to south.

Down the street, he heard the crack of a Winchester .30-.30.

Raider almost didn't see it.

He never reached the blue roan tied to the south side of the street.

Instead, he was distracted by something on the north side.

A brief flash of light, as the first rays of the sun glanced off a gun barrel.

Instinctively, he ducked and drew his pistol.

The rifle barrel jutted from between two buildings. As Raider stared at it, he saw it belch flame and heard it crack like a whip. A puff of dust kicked up five yards from him, peppering his legs.

The rifle barrel swung upward. The rifle barked again. The bullet hissed past Raider's ear as he went into a fighting crouch, his hammer cocked. He fired and knew he had missed even as he squeezed the trigger.

Chunks of splintered wood flew off the building, inches higher than the rifle barrel.

He heard the cocking mechanism of the Winchester.

"Raider, throw down your gun."

Big Jake's voice boomed across the street.

Raider answered with a quick shot, low this time, and wide. He shook his head and looked for cover.

The Winchester spoke again, and Raider felt a tug at his sleeve. The bullet ripped through cloth, singing his left forearm.

Close. Too damned close.

There was no place to hide.

Big Jake cocked the Winchester again.

Raider knew his chances were slim. He made a decision. If he ran away, he would be shot down like a dog. If he hit the dirt, he'd be a still target. He ran.

Straight toward Big Jake's hiding place.

He fired on the run, zigzagging.

The Winchester '73 boomed. Dirt stung Raider's legs. He fired again, keeping count of the bullets now. His and Big Jake's.

He held his fire and dove for the building on the left. He hit the ground hard and rolled as another rifle shot shattered his eardrums. A jarring pain rocketed through his shoulder, where he had landed. His left arm couldn't take much more punishment. He hugged the building and brought his pistol up.

Loman would have to step out and expose himself to get in another shot.

"Raider?" Big Jake's voice was low, almost a whisper.

"Yeah?"

"Can we make a deal?"

"I doubt it."

"It's just you and me."

Raider heard him shoving fresh shells into the chamber. He held his pistol steady on the opening between the buildings.

"I can make you rich," said Loman. "Gold. Not many to split it with now. You can go to Mexico, live out your days in luxury."

"Where's the gold, Loman?"

"In the mine. Lorelei's there now with Abernathy, loading it up. There's still about fifty thousand in silver dollars, too. Not Pecos dollars but genuine Morgans."

Loman finished loading. Raider listened hard and heard the hammer go back. He smiled. Big Jake had pulled the trigger slightly to release the tension so he wouldn't hear the rifle cock. But Raider heard the faint click as the trigger mechanism locked into the sear.

"I might be interested," he said softly. "How do you want to work it?"

"We both put our guns down, right between the buildings. Where we can both see them."

"Tricky. Who goes first?"

"We do it on the count of three. I'll slide my barrel down the wall so you can see it."

"All right," said Raider.

The rifle barrel jutted out beyond the side of the building. It started to slide slowly down toward the ground.

Raider waddled on his haunches toward the edge of the building. He reached up, grabbed the end of the barrel, and jerked. He pulled it free of Big Jake's hands. It was easy. Too easy. Raider dropped the rifle quickly and threw himself on his back between the buildings.

Big Jake fired his pistol point-blank at the point where he believed Raider to be.

When he saw Raider looking up at him, it was too late.

Raider fired a bullet into Jake's crotch.

Big Jake screamed and dropped his pistol.

Raider stood up, smoke streaming from the barrel of his Remington .44.

Loman sagged to the ground, his face drained of blood. The big-caliber ball had ripped into his testicles, churning them to pulp.

"My god, what have you done to me?" gasped Big Jake.

"Shot your balls off, you bastard."

"No!"

"If you stop the bleeding, Loman, you might live," said Raider. "But you'll talk in a high, squeaky voice."

Raider left him there, holding on to the bloody remnants of his manhood. He ran to the blue roan and hauled himself into the saddle.

He didn't turn around, but he heard a pistol shot a few seconds later.

A single pistol shot that seemed to echo in his ears for a long time after the sound died away.

Abernathy set the box of dynamite against the wall of the mine. Lorelei unreeled ten minutes of fuse.

She opened the box and took out a single stick. She shoved a blasting cap down into the pulpy sawdust that was laced with nitroglycerin. She wore gloves, knowing the gelatin could give her a headache if she rubbed her forehead with hands that had come in contact with the paraffin coating the paper.

She shoved the end of the fuse into the cap and crimped it with her teeth.

"You know your business," said Abernathy.

"I learned it from Big Jake."

"Where is he? We're all loaded. I heard shots."

"Maybe he took care of Raider. Better go outside and get the team ready, Josiah. I'll light this fuse and be with you in a minute."

"I'll wait. I'm nervous. I can't stand to think of those people burning to death."

"Your weak stomach will get you killed someday," she said curtly. She struck a match and lit the fuse. "There won't be a trace of this phony mine once that box goes off."

The burning fuse hissed like a snake. Shadows danced on the walls of the cave.

"Come on," she said. "Let's find Big Jake."

Instead they found Raider, waiting for them outside the mine entrance.

"You armed, Abernathy?"

"No, I'm not."

Raider stood by the wagon, seemingly at ease. He looked at the pistol on Lorelei's hip, the big-bladed bowie knife in its sheath.

"Step away, then, and keep your hands where I can see them."

Abernathy stepped several paces away from Lorelei. He glanced back at the mine and opened his mouth to say something.

"Shut up, Josiah," said Lorelei.

Seconds ticked away.

"But the—"

"I said shut up," she snapped.

"What's the matter, Lorelei?"

"There's a lot of gold still in the mine," she said. "It's yours if you let us go."

"That's the second time today I got offered a bribe. Big Jake's offer didn't work either."

"Damn you!"

"Now, now, Lorelei," he said. "Don't be cursing me. I'm going to give you your choices. Two U.S. marshals are on their way here. Doc and I have orders to detain you and Abernathy by force if necessary. You can either drop that gunbelt or see if you can outdraw me."

"You'd shoot a woman?"

"I'd shoot you, lady."

"What kind of man are you? Don't you care about the finer things in life? We could go south together and live in splendor. If Big Jake's dead, there's just you and me and Abernathy. Over a million dollars between the three of us. Can you explain why a man would turn down riches? I could love you, make you happy. Am I not desirable? Wouldn't any man give anything to sleep with me? If you have any explanation why my offer doesn't appeal to you, I wish you'd tell me."

"Fuck you, Lorelei," he explained.

Abernathy, sweat breaking over his forehead, his hands shaking, could no longer stand the tension. The dynamite would go off any minute now. He opened his coat and reached for a small-caliber pistol concealed in his watch pocket.

Raider saw the move.

His hand streaked for his pistol like a bird's shadow.

Abernathy got his fingers on the derringer.

Lorelei's eyes widened when she saw how fast Raider was. His pistol was out, bucking in his hand, before she could move.

Abernathy jerked as the first bullet struck his chest. He aimed the derringer and cocked it. Raider's second shot blew out an eye, squishing it like a grape. Abernathy's scream was cut off as the ball burned a furrow through his brain. He fell, blood streaming from the empty eye socket, a hole in the back of his head the size of a saucer.

Lorelei ran back into the mine.

Raider loped after her.

Behind him he heard a yell as Doc and two men rode up on horseback.

"Get her, Raider!"

Raider dashed into the dark cavern. He heard a whispering sound. He ducked, and Lorelei's pistol barrel glanced off his skull. He grappled with her. They staggered deeper into the mine. Her pistol fell from her hand.

He heard the hiss before he saw the sparkling end of the fuse. Fire raced along the timed fuse, shortening it.

Lorelei was strong. She tried to knee him in the groin. He warded off the blow and drove a fist into her side. She twisted free and tried to dart past him. He hurled himself at her in a flying tackle.

They went down. Lorelei bit his arm and scratched at his eyes.

Raider lashed out with his right fist and struck her in the left temple. She got to her feet and kicked him in the mouth. His head shot back from the force of the blow.

The fuse hissed on.

Raider leaped to his feet and chased Lorelei. He holstered his pistol and dove for her again.

They crashed to the floor of the cave.

Lorelei's fingers gouged at his eyes.

He drove her away with a bull rush that brought him to his feet. He grabbed her by the hair and dragged her to the mind entrance.

"Let me up," she gasped.

He helped her to her feet, sure that the fight was all out of her.

Doc and the marshals started toward the mine.

"Stay away!" yelled Raider. "Dynamite! The fuse is lit."

Before he realized it, Lorelei broke away from him and dashed back into the mine. He started after her. Doc rushed up, grabbed Raider by the collar, and jerked him back.

"Don't go in there!" he said.

"Doc, she doesn't have time to put out that fuse!"

He was interrupted by the thundering explosion. Smoke and dust billowed out of the cave. The blast knocked the Pinkertons down, showering them with a powdery grit. Small stones bounced all around them as they covered their heads.

Then there was only a terrible silence.

The marshals took possession of the gold and silver.

Grabowski sat sullenly in their wagon, his wrists and ankles in irons. Of all the bandits, it was ironic that he was the only one left alive. He had no brains, only muscle, and Doc had worked him over pretty well. Purple bruises blotched his face; his lips were swollen, cracked, caked with blood.

Doc made the women comfortable in his wagon. Raider finished checking the cinches on the blue roan.

"Wonder if you fellows heard the bad news?" said Marshal Edward Wales, a balding man in his forties.

"Nope," said Raider.

"The country's in a depression. Silver isn't worth a damned thing, and the foreign markets ran us out of gold reserves."

"That so?" asked Doc.

"Yep," said Goode. "India stopped making silver coins, and I reckon we will too."

"Then those Pecos dollars and the Morgans might be worth some money someday," said Doc.

"Doubt it. You can't give silver away," said Wales.

"Too bad," said Raider. "I felt rich there for a few minutes."

People streamed away from the empty town. Most of it had been saved from burning, but nothing could save it from death. Smoke from charred ashes rose in dark plumes as Doc clucked to Judith, following the marshals in their wagon full of gold and worthless silver coins.

Raider looked back at the smoldering town and spat in the dirt.

The blue roan switched its tail and stepped out in a frisky canter.

"Come see me in Santa Fe," said Laura Lee, her head sticking out of the back of Doc's medicine wagon.

"I'll do that," said Raider with a wide grin. "Right soon."

Then he put spurs to the roan's flanks and raced ahead, as if to put distance between him and Pecos Gulch.

His pocket jingled with two shiny Pecos dollars.

He drew them out and sailed them into the air, one at a time.

They disappeared into the rocks and brush of an empty, desolate land, worthless souvenirs of a dead town that should never have been born.